A Garland Series

Foundations of the Novel

Representative Early

Eighteenth-Century Fiction

A collection of 100 rare titles
reprinted in photo-facsimile in 71 volumes

Foundations of the Novel

compiled and edited by

Michael F. Shugrue

Secretary for English for the M.L.A.

with New Introductions for each volume by

Michael Shugrue, *City College of C.U.N.Y.*

Malcolm J. Bosse, *City College of C.U.N.Y.*

William Graves, *N.Y. Institute of Technology*

Josephine Grieder, *Rutgers University, Newark*

The Generous Rivals
Or, Love Triumphant

Anonymous

with a new introduction
for the Garland Edition by
Malcolm J. Bosse

Garland Publishing, Inc., New York & London

1973

The new introduction for the

Garland *Foundations of the Novel* Edition

is Copyright © 1973, by

Garland Publishing, Inc., New York & London

All Rights Reserved

Bibliographical note:

*This facsimile has been made from a copy in the
British Museum
(12614.ccc.1)*

Library of Congress Cataloging in Publication Data
Main entry under title:

The Generous rivals.

(Foundations of the novel)
Reprint of the 1713 ed., printed for J. Morphew,
London.
I. Title: Love triumphant. II. Series.
PZ3.G28653 1973 [PR3291.A1] 823'.5 72-170531
ISBN 0-8240-0532-5

Printed in the United States of America

Introduction

The Generous Rivals *is an intricate ballet of manners, a romantic novel which follows the comic formula of reshaping relationships among lovers through the media of their misunderstandings. True to the sentimental tone of the story, the language is grandiloquent, but at times its controlled employment of rhetorical devices, especially antithesis, elevates it linguistically above many of the eighteenth-century examples of this genre.*

Dorinda, orphaned at fifteen, is a paragon of beauty and virtue, whose charms attract a number of aristocratic suitors. Old Vulpone, her uncle and miserly guardian, decides that Phylastratus is the best among them because of his wealth. When Dorinda fails to show him special favor, Phylastratus seeks the advice of his friend, Panaretus, who ascribes her coolness to "the common Caprice of her Sex" (p. 8). When on behalf of his friend Panaretus speaks to her, Dorinda promptly falls in love with him, thus providing the conflict for the first and better half of the novel. Dialogues of cross-purpose ensue, which are based upon a misinterpretation of Dorinda's choice of lover; these errors of communication are handled skillfully enough, although without the sparkling wit that Sheridan would bring to such matters in his plays later in the century. Love makes Dorinda lose all propriety, a typical consequence of passion in the view of eighteenth-century roman-

ticists, and she throws herself recklessly at Panaretus, who proves too much the gentleman to take advantage of her or of his trusting friend. Struck by Panaretus' honorable steadfastness, Phylastratus decides to give up his own suit and bring the two lovers together. The ensuing machinations develop principally through letters, an epistolary technique of interest because Phylastratus follows the progress of the romance by acting as messenger and shapes events by reading the letters which he delivers. The narrative pace is blunted, however, by the insertion of a long pastoral poem, written by Panaretus at Dorinda's urging. It presents in dull verse the conventional theme of the lovelorn: "A Lovers Bliss, is all an idle Dream" (p. 90).

A subsidiary plot begins when Phylastratus attempts to prove that Caelia, his friend's fiancee, is an opportunist without scruples. The psychological transitions by which the quartet of lovers changes allegiance are admirably handled for a romantic novel. Once Caelia's falseness is revealed, the two friends are fully reconciled and the two lovers declare their passion. The plot veers again when Dorinda asks Panaretus "whether she was the first ever had the Happiness of gaining his Affections" (p. 148), and he replies with an account of his affair with Caelia, which forms an inset story entitled "The Amours of Panaretus and Caelia." The author tries to contrast true and false notions of love and to warn against the impassioned imagination, which betrays people in love: "Luxuriant Fancy painted her so extravagantly pleasing to every Sense, that I thought it

INTRODUCTION

cou'd never sufficiently dilate upon her" (p. 160). The point is made, appropriately enough for a romance, that poor breeding and insufficient education account for deceit during courtship.

Once again the narrative shifts, this time to the activities of the greedy Vulpone, whom the high-spirited trio conspire to fool. The avaricious uncle then obstructs the course of true love by demanding that Panaretus stop seeing his ward. The young man leaves the country to make his fortune and Dorinda, in despair, runs away from home. Vulnerable in the outside world, she soon is caught in the wicked designs of a young rake. The beleaguered girl and her seducer debate at length the morality of sexual freedom, the legal and emotional consequences of adultery, and the viability of family life. No Lovelace, the rake is humbled by her arguments, especially after her threat that if he did not "immediately desist his base and ungenerous Carriage, she wou'd alarm the House" (p. 232). Upon Panaretus' return from war, which in a subtle technical decision is not described, he rediscovers Dorinda in a highly coincidental manner. They marry and retire to a country seat on money recovered from Vulpone. The last sentence of the novel points the moral in a paradigm of the genre: "Happiness, real substantial Happiness, is only to be found in Innocence and Vertue."

In spite of his initial dexterity in handling the plot, the author fails to sustain the kind of emotional intensity which distinguishes the work of Richardson and some of his followers, especially that of Charlotte

7

INTRODUCTION

Smith. The constant need to recharge the plot reveals the author's inability to find the emotional center of his characters and then to rely upon motivation from within for the development of interesting situations. On the other hand, The Generous Rivals *is a cut above the average sentimental eighteenth-century novel, and at times the rhetorical prose carries within its balanced phrases a solid insight into character:*

> *So far was he from that abject Narrowness of Spirit which determines all its Acts of Kindness within the little Circle of Self-Interest; that he took a sort of generous Pride, not only in being Friendly, but in hiding it when he had done. (p. 126)*

Malcolm J. Bosse

THE
GENEROUS RIVALS:
OR,
LOVE
TRIUMPHANT.
A
NOVEL.

Res est soliciti plena Timoris Amor.

Ovid.

LONDON·

Printed for J. Morphew, near Stationer's-Hall, 1713.

THE
Generous Rivals,
OR
Love Triumphant.

I SHALL not trouble you with the splendid Titles of our Heroin's Anceſtors; nor attempt to recount the ſeveral Marks of Dignity in their Scutcheons; but content my ſelf with acquainting you, that both her Father and Mother, were of a genteel Extract: And made it their continu'd Study, whilſt they liv'd, to qualify their Daughter, to keep up to the Character. It were needleſs alſo to amuſe you with a Recital of the indul-

B　　　　　　gent

gent Affection her Father bore Her;
and the various impulsive Fore-Bode-
ings her Mother had, of her being to
act some extraordinary Part; with a-
bundance of other such curious Remarks
which are generally made, the better
to grace an Introduction of this Kind.
Neither shall I Essay to warm your I-
magination, by an elaborate Description of her many personal Perfections:
But let it suffice, only to inform you,
that she was Beauteous enough to attract the Affections of most of the adjacent Youths of any Character, and
Witty enough so to manage her Charms,
as to fix some endearing Ideas of her
extraordinary Merits, on the Minds of
all that saw her; and leave the following Pages to expatiate on the Rest of
her Character.

No sooner had Time usher'd in the
Fifteenth Year of her Age, but Heaven,
for wise Ends, known to its self only,
depriv'd her in the Space of one Month,
of both her Parents; and thereby at
once gave her the unhappy Appellation
of

of Orphan, and her Unkle the *Defpotic*
One of Guardian. This fhocking Stroke
made fuch fenfible, and accute Impreffions on her Mind, for almoft a whole
Year following : That fhe wholly a-
bandon'd all Company, and feem'd inclin'd to Nothing, but the feveral Enter-
tainments of a Reclufe. All poffible
Endeavours were made to divert this
her folitary Temper, both by her
Unkle, and all her Intimates ; but their
utmoft Arts prov'd all fruftrate, 'till
Time began by leifure Degrees, to
erace the melancholly Ideas of her
Misfortunes out of her Mind.

Luna having undergone Twelve di-
ftinct Mutations, and Cuftom calling
for her Difcharge of her Sable : She began with her Cloaths, to refume by
little, and little, her wonted Gaiety of
Temper, and in fhort time became fuch
an abfolute Artift in the Politic's of *Cupid*,
as to gain the unanimous Admiration of
the Male, and univerfal Envy of her
own Sex. She appear'd fo every way
Lovely in the Eye of the One; and fo

I know not how, worthy to be found fault with by the Other; that she was a continu'd Subject for Conversation to all about her.

Dorinda finding her self so unverfally carress'd, quickly made those Advantages of her Circumstances, as is common to her Sex; and so artfully manag'd her Eyes, that with the greatest Facility imaginable she made all the Fools her Slaves, and Wife-men her Fools, within Sight of her. Go where you wou'd, *Dorinda* was the Theme; if there was any Airs at a Ball, peculiarly graceful, 'twas like *Dorinda*; was there any Part in a Play, more than ordinary ingaging, 'twas like *Dorinda*. Where-ever she went, she seem'd to command Respect; and all about her appear'd to have no other Notion of Happiness, but by being some Way or other serviceable to her. Here was One, striving to invert Nature, and his Brains gingling like so many Bells; curfing (instead of invoking) the Muses, for not thrusting elegant Nonfenfe e-
no ugh

nough into his Pate, to make a Panegyric : There another wracking Con-
science, turning Occafional Conformift,
any thing but Honeft, to get Money
enough to barter with her Unkle, knowing if his Money did not, his Merits'
wou'd never recommend him. In fine,
to gain her Favour, was efteem'd the
Summum bonum, by all the Young *Cy-*
prians round her ; and all they did,
or thought, was no otherways good
or reafonable, than as it conduc'd to
the gaining of her good Opinion.

Her Unkle ftrictly obferving the
Crowd of Suitors, that were continually making their Addreffes to his Neice ;
foon began (with a Temper common
to Old-Age) to think of fome Meafures,
that might turn this to his own Intereft,
and thereupon immediately began to
weigh, not the Merits, but Advantages
her feveral Sparks had in Fortune, above
each Other ; and finding the Reafons
of this Kind, abundantly turn the Bal-
lance, in Favour of *Phylaftratus*, a
Young Gentleman, who had enter'd

the Lift of *Dorinda*'s Admirers, prefently concluded her his Property, and cafhier'd, without any further Confideration, all the Reft.

Phylaftratus, not infenfible of the Advantage he had gain'd, immediately made his Addreffes to *Dorinda*, with all the Gallantry and Exaltednefs of Mien, which is peculiar to the Politeft Gentlemen of the Age, and was receiv'd by her, with an Air of Complaifance, fo uncommonly Graceful; as at once made him paffionately defire her Favour, and admire her Prudence. Her Carriage was in its every Part, fo free from the common Affectation of her Sex; and her Converfe fo much rais'd above their ufual Impertinences; fo ingagingly expreſive of the moft exalted Modefty, and yet, fo wholly void of all Caprice; that it at once difcharg'd her of both thofe common Imputations upon the Ladies, too eafy Fondnefs, or imperious Incivility.

Whilft *Phylaftratus* thus repeatedly continu'd his Vifits to *Dorinda*, Old
Vulpone

Vulpone, her Unkle, inceſſantly im-ploy'd his Thoughts upon ſome Me-thods of advancing his Bags; and to that end took all Opportunities, largely to inculcate what an extraordinary Zeal he had imploy'd in the Intereſt of him; particularly urging the Pains he had taken to ingratiate him into his Neice's Favour, not forgetting eſpeci-ally to give him ſome ſhrew'd Hints of the many, and great Gratuities; thoſe he had deny'd upon his Account, offer'd him for a like Freedom of Acceſs.

Phylaſtratus caſily gueſſing, what *Vulpone* drove at, by Haranges of this Nature; and having a Fortune that rais'd him above the Want, as well as a Mind too generous to deſire any thing that *Dorinda*'s Fortune cou'd furniſh him with, of that Nature; ſoon gave Him ſuch guilded Indications, that he wou'd not be ungrateful in that Kind, as riveted his avaritious Soul intirely to his Intereſt.

Having thus fully ſatisfied *Vulpone,* and repeated his Addreſſes, now for the space of a whole Month, and finding *Do-rinda* return'd even his greateſt Aſſidui-ties, in no other manner, than by face-tious Perverſions, and Punctilious Cere-monies: He began to have ſome little Uneaſineſs at the Inconſiderableneſs of his Progreſs ; and being of a Soul too Maſculine, and exalted, to be Coxcomb Couchant, to Beauty Rampant ; com-municated the whole Matter to *Pa-naretus,* a Young Gentleman, his par-ticular Intimate (who had made him privy to an Affair of his of the ſame Nature, a little before) and deſir'd his Advice in the Matter.

Panaretus having fully weigh'd the Account, *Phylaſtratus* had given him of his Amour, and being by his Acquain-tance with him, ſufficiently prepoſſeſs'd with a favourable Opinion of his Merits, immediately imputed *Dorinda*'s ſeem-ing Declining of his Suit, to be the Effect of the common Caprice of her Sex ; and therefore bid him baniſh all Doubts in the Matter, and not fear, his Endeavours being crown'd with a Succeſs equal to,
even

even to the utmoſt of his Wiſhes : Adding, that if he cou'd have the Honour to ſee her, he did not doubt making ſuch Diſcoveries, as wou'd afford him an intire Satisfaction.

Phylaſtratus being thus animated by his Friend, promis'd the next time he paid a Viſit to his Miſtreſs, he ſhou'd accompany him, deſiring him to make the utmoſt Remarks of her Carriage he poſſibly cou'd ; and to omit nothing that the moſt induſtrious Sagacity cou'd contribute to gain Intelligence of her Inclinations. *Panaretus* promis'd to be ſtrictly obſervant of his Inſtructions; and accordingly fixt a Time to attend him, to reduce them to Practice; and ſoon after went with him to pay her Unkle a Viſit, with a Mind wholly reſolv'd to uſe all poſſible Arts to recommend his Friend.

Vulpone receiv'd them with all the ſlaviſh Obeſequiouſneſs that is common to Souls of a mercenary and abject Nature.; and knowing, (tho' he was the Pretence, his Neice's Company

B 5   was

was the thing defir'd) immediately convey'd them both into her Appartment, there leaving them, true *Pandar* like, to make their own Apology.

No fooner were they enter'd, but the Room difplay'd the agreeable Scene of *Dorinda,* and her Maid *Ifabella,* at the Exercife of their Needle. Their fudden Appearance gave fome little Surprize to *Dorinda,* and caus'd fuch a plentiful Effufion of the Rofe all over her Face, as gave an engaging Luftre to her native Beauties : But Education, and her natural Sweetnefs of Temper having rais'd her above being, at any time, guilty of any Incivility : She foon refum'd her ufual Sweetnefs of Addrefs, and after common Ceremonies had pafs'd, defir'd them to fit down ; with which they both very readily comply'd.

Being feated, *Phylaftratus* told her, " his Friend *Panaretus* and he, coming " by her Houfe, immediately ingag'd " in Difpute about her, and as was " very common amongft Difputants ;
they

" they had carry'd the Conteſt ſo
" far as to render it impoſſible to
" bring it to an Iſſue, without an
" Appeal to a Third Perſon ; and
" after a ſhort Debate had agreed ſhe
" ſhou'd give the deciſive Sentence.
Dorinda reply'd, " She was not old
" enough ſhe thought for a Judge, or
" at leaſt ſhe was very ambitious ; and
" therefore did not think it worth her
" while to interpoſe in ſo inconſiderable
" a Subjeᴄt, as ſhe found they were in-
" gag'd in ; adding, that if ſhe ever
" took upon her, that awful Poſt,
" it ſhou'd be in a Matter of
" ſome Importance, and not in any
" thing that had Relation to ſuch a
" ſimple inſignificant Girl, as *Dorin-*
" *da* ; who was fit, only to exerciſe
" the Levity of a Buffoon ; but cou'd
" never be thought a proper Imploy-
" ment for the Debates of one that bore
" ſo auguſt a Name, as that of Judge.
Panaretus finding his Comrade ſo wittily rally'd by his Miſtreſs ; ſaid, " As to
" the Diſpute, mention'd by *Phylaſtratus,*
" he

" he did not much infift on't, but he
" verily thought the feeing and hear-
" ing of her, wou'd commence fuch a
" fort of Debate between them, as all
" their preceeding Friendfhip wou'd
" not be able to put an end to. I am
" not (faid he) fo ftupidly infenfible of
" the moft exalted Felicity this lower
" Orb can produce, not to know that
" there is fomething in every Part of a
" Lady like *Dorinda,* that deferves a
" Conteft ; and therefore *Phylaftratus*
" will have no great Reafon to be fur-
" priz'd if a Platonick Flame be fuper-
" ceeded by another of fuperiour Force,
" at moft he might blame his own Fol-
" ly, for giving the Temptation.——I
" am not fo unacquainted (anfwer'd *Do-*
" *rinda,* interrupting him) with the
" natural Gallantry of *Phylaftratus,* as
" not eafily to infer, that One who
" has contracted fo particular an Inti-
" macy with him (as you, Sir, I find
" have done) has a large Share of the
" fame Qualities, and therefore I am
" not much furpriz'd, to find my felf
                    " accofted

" accosted with so many Aulicisms;
" but yet, methinks I can't but make
" this Complaint (my whole Sex being
" really concern'd in it) that so much
" Wit, and Eloquence, shou'd always be
" imploy'd by you Young Gentlemen,
" in the Ladies Company, purely to
" render us more vain; and conse-
" quently, more contemptable Crea-
" tures than even Heaven it self
" design'd us. *Phylastratus* going to
make reply, was interrupted by *Valpo-
ne*, who agreeable to preceeding Appointment, call'd him out, telling him
he wanted to speak with him.

Panaretus being thus abandon'd by
his Companion, and left alone with *Dorinda*, easily apprehended his Business;
and therefore us'd all the Art he was
Master of, to introduce some Discourse
with her, about *Phylastratus*; telling
her they were School-Fellows, and not
forgetting (with a seeming Indifference
of Air) to inform her of the bright As-
cendancy he soon gain'd over the rest
of his Fellow *Pupils*, in all the several
Parts

Parts of useful Learning, artfully recounting the many little Intriegues of their Juvenile Years, in which *Phylaſtratus* was ſure to be repreſented, as acting ſome Part, which wou'd neceſſarily afford Matter for Encomium. In fine, his Generoſity, Wit, Education, and all that *Panaretus*, cou'd think Praiſe worthy, was ſet off, with all the Beauty and Grace, that Wit, Eloquence, and Friendſhip, cou'd poſſibly dictate to him; and nothing was omitted that cou'd contribute, to convey the moſt Beautiful Ideas of his Perfections into her Mind.

Dorinda finding herſelf ſo generouſly harangu'd by *Panaretus*, in Behalf of his Friend, was ſo ſenſibly impreſs'd by the Charms of his Elocution, and found the uſual Pregnancy of her Wit, ſo unaccountably retarded, as render'd her wholly incapable, of returning him any other Anſwer, than Bluſhes, and broken and inarticulate Expreſſions. The various Beauties of his Rehetoric, and the winning Accents of his Tongue

had

had fuch a ftrange afcendancy over all her Faculties, and caus'd fuch violent Emotions, and Perturbations in her Breaft ; as perfectly manacl'd the wonted Vivacity of her *Genius*, and render'd her utmoft endeavours, unable to hide her Diforder. Under this unaccuftom'd Perplexity, fhe found her felf in a perfect Laborinth ; wholly unable to fpeak, and yet not knowing well how to be filent : But being apprehenfive, *Panaretus* wou'd take Cognizance of the Concern fhe was under, fhe rally'd her utmoft Power to carry it off, and finding her felf altogether, incapable to hide it, intreated him not to take it amifs, that fhe did not feem to give that Attendance to what he had faid, it merited, becaufe fhe was taken at prefent fomething ill, and defir'd him further to excufe her retiring out of the Room ; and accordingly fhe retir'd.

Panaretus having ftrictly obferv'd the many Changes in *Dorinda's* Countenance, during his Difcourfe with her ; conftru'd it all in Favour of his Friend

Phy-

Phylaſtratus, and. mightily delighted himſelf with the Satisfaction, the Account of his Proceedings, wou'd afford him. He imputed all the Diſorder in her Looks, and Abruptneſs in her Words, to be the Effect of the Mention of *Phylaſtratus*'s Name, and the preſent Illneſs ſhe ſeem'd to be ſeized with, the Reſult only, of a ſort of Tranſport, to find Another have the ſame Senſe of his Perfections, as her ſelf. In ſhort, his Mind was ſo fully poſſeſs'd with a noble Simpathy in what he thought wou'd conduce to the Happineſs of his Friend ; that he was quite impatient 'till he had an Opportunity to give him (as he thought) a grateful Account of his Management.

On the other ſide, *Dorinda* having, after her leaving *Panaretus*, lockt her ſelf up in her Cloſet, found the Commotion he had rais'd in her Breaſt ſtill continue, and ſuch a Miſcellany of Pleaſure and Pain, attend the Reflection upon what had paſs'd between Them, as render'd her utmoſt Reſolution too

we ak

weak to encounter, and repel it. There
was fomething within her, that plead-
ed with fuch irrefiftable Oratory, in
Favour of *Panaretus*, and drefs'd up
his every Part in fuch beautiful, and ingaging Forms, as made her Imagination unable to forbear making Inlargc-
ments upon him. The Sprightlinefs of
his Mien, the Pregnancy, and yet, un-
affectednefs of his Wit, the fincere and
generous Zeal he fhow'd for his Friend,
with the numerous Crowd of his other
excellent Qualities, made fuch indeli-
ble Impreffions on her Soul, as put
her under an impoffibility of ceafing to
think on him. She found her felf, by I
know not what fatal Neceffity, forc'd
to lodge him with a more than common Kindnefs, in her Breaft, and her
Heart, in Contempt of all Oppofition,
wou'd declare him Welcome. He appear'd fo tranfcendantly exalted above
the reft of Mankind, and they, when
oppofs'd to him, even in their moft fhining Qualifications, fo ftrangely dull
and infipid, that fhe cou'd not but think
on,

on, and thinking on, love and admire him. His obliging Addreſs perfectly riveted her Soul to the Contemplation of him, and the many Beauties of his Converſe monopoliz'd her whole Thoughts.

Whilſt *Panaretus* and *Dorinda* were thus differently affected with what had paſs'd between them : *Vulpone* was very buſily employ'd, in telling *Phylaſtratus* how Zealous he had been in his Service, ſaying he had omitted no endeavours to advance his Intereſt with his Neice ; and that *Phylaſtratus* might not be Inſenſible of the many mighty things he had done for him, Enumerated all the particulars of his Converſe with *Dorinda*, and mention'd every thing that had paſs'd, tho' never ſo Triffling, and Impertinent : 'Till *Phylaſtratus* quite tir'd with the tediouſneſs of his Ignorance, and under the moſt eager deſire of knowing how *Panaretus* had manag'd matters with *Dorinda* ; told him, he thought it now high time, to go and give *Panaretus*
and

and *Dorinda* a Vifit, and thereupon
rofe and went immediately to the
Room where he left *Dorinda*, and his
Correfpondent *Panaretus.*

Coming into the Room and finding
Dorinda gone, and *Panaretus* fitting in
a mufing Pofture, he Smil'd and faid,
" So *Panaretus*, you're abandon'd by the
" Lady I find : I fancy your Embaffy
" has not been attended with that Suc-
" cefs you had conceiv'd of it. You
" have the priviledge of Laughing I
" confefs, (anfwer'd *Panaretus*) becaufe
" you have Won. Won ! (cry'd *Phy-*
" *laftratus*) what Pray ? A Prize faid
" *Panaretus*, I fear will make you Co-
" veteous. In fhort *Phylaftratus*, I
" won't fay a Word more except you
" Hire me. I never took you to be
" Mercenary before ; (faid *Phylaftratus*)
" But prithee tell me, what did She
" fay ? Say ! (anfwer'd *Panaretus*) no-
" thing. She Sigh'd, Blufh'd, fell Sick at
" the bare mention of your Name ; and
" I'll fwear, made as pretty a Victim to
" the little God as ever you faw. De-
" pend

" pend on't She Loves you. Does She?
" said *Phylaſtratus*, then I'll Love Her,
" and upon other Conditions, was *Hel-*
" *len* her ſelf my Miſtreſs, I wou'd
" not ſpend an Irkſome Thought a-
" bout Her. But yet when all is done,
" thou haſt a ſtrange Faculty *Panaretus*
" of making the Ladies Bluſh, where-
" ever you go : For my Part, the ut-
" moſt Range of Fancy I was Maſter
" of ever ſince I knew Her, never had
" that Effect ; if there was any Bluſh-
" ing, I'll ſwear 'twas on my ſide, to
" find my ſelf always ſo Wittily Baffl'd,
" even at my own Weapons, by one we
" Pride our ſelves, in calling of the weak-
" er Sex. I found ſomething in Her
" Genius, ſo particularly Nimble, that
" let me do what I wou'd, I cou'd ne're
" be quick enough for it. She'd Anti-
" cipate my very Thoughts, and An-
" ſwer me before I ſpoke. Lovers
" you know (reply'd *Panaretus*) are al-
" ways Blind, and therefore 'tis no
" wonder, Her Bluſhes were not percep-
" tible to you. You was always under
" too

"too much diſorder your ſelf, to be
" capable of making any Diſcoveries
" in Her. You're a ſad Fellow, *Pana-*
" *retus*, (ſaid *Phylaſtratus*) I ſhall ſee
" you ſome time or other again with
" your *Cælia*, and then ! Aye then,
" (anſwer'd *Panaretus*) you'll ſee me as
" Blind as you are. Was it not for that
" only Conſideration, I think verily I
" ſhould endeavour, to Rival you.
Upon which, *Phylaſtratus* looking
upon his Watch, ſaid 'twas paſt Ten
a Clock : So they agreed to call
Iſabella, and order her to preſent
both of their humble Services to her
Miſtreſs, and tell her, they wiſh'd
her a good Repoſe. *Iſabella* agreeable to their Deſire, informing *Do-*
rinda they were going, She bid her
tell them ſhe wou'd come to them
immediately ; and accordingly appear'd,
and bid Them both good Night.

Having thus parted with *Dorinda* and
her Unkle, *Panaretus* gave his Friend
a thorough Account of his Conference
with Her : Telling him he thought
all

all the Circumſtances of it, ſeem'd to Concur to his Advantage, and if the making *Dorinda* his Bride, was the thing he deſir'd, he did not doubt ſee. ing it Effected in a reaſonable Time; bidding him have ſome Regard to the Proverb, and not let the want of Courage above all things be charg'd upon him. *Phylaſtratus* being thus Encourag'd by his Friend's Relation, told him he ſhou'd take an Opportunity very ſoon, of Acting agreeable to his Advice.

Accordingly, next Day he went to pay *Dorinda* a Viſit, and to his Surprize, found her ſtrangely chang'd in Her Countenance. The wonted ſprightlineſs of her Mien, was apparantly eſtrang'd, and her every Part carry'd with it, ſome evident Symtoms of inward Diſcontent. There was a ſort of ſecret Inquietude, which diſplay'd it ſelf in all She did or ſaid, and tho' She made her utmoſt Efforts, She could not poſſibly hide her Diſorder. Her Face was one continu'd Scene of Revolution: And there ſeem'd a ſort of Emulation between

tween the *Rofe* and *Lilly*, which fhou'd
moft difcover her Concern. The Lovely Idea, She had Form'd of *Panaretus's*
Perfections, had fo ftrangely deprefs'd
the native Brisknefs of her Difpofition, that She cou'd not fo much as appear Chearful. *Phylaftratus* obferving
" the Perplexity *Dorinda* was in, ask'd
" her whether She was well? No
" Sir, faid She I am not very well. I
" wifh Madam, he reply'd, it lay in my
" Power to make you well; fo do I too,
anfwer'd She, but that's Impoffible.

   Phylaftratus finding himfelf Anfwer'd,
with this Melancholy fort of Ambigu-
ty of Expreffion by *Dorinda*, continu'd
the Difcourfe with all the Art He poffibly cou'd; ufing all the little Turns of
Whim and Fancy he cou'd think on, to
gain Intelligence of the Caufes of her
prefent vifible Alteration; 'till finding
all his Endeavours fail him, and all her
Anfwers, if they carry'd any thing of
her ufual Chearfulnefs in them, purely,
the Effect of a kind of forc'd and penfive Civility; he bethought himfelf to
make

make mention of *Panaretus,* " Telling
" her that he faw him juft before he
" came to her, and that he Preffingly
" defir'd him to prefent his humble Ser-
" vice to her.   The fo unexpected mention of. *Panaretus*'s Name, immediately caus'd a very vifible Emotion in her
Breaft, and the feveral changes in her
Countenance, foon made *Phylaftratus*
difcover, fhe had a more than Common Regard to him.   The very found
of it, bore fuch fweet Harmony with her
Heart, that fhe was no longer able to
hide the Evidences of her inward diftur-
bance, from appearing in her Looks ;
nor *Phylaftratus,* who ftrictly remark'd
her carriage, any more to feek for the
Caufe of her Diforder.

Having by this odd turn, gain'd fuch
an unexpected Intelligence of her Inclinations : He immediately refolv'd
to Difemble his having any Apprehen-
fion of the Matter, that he might have
the better Opportunity of knowing all
Paffages, that he cou'd not but forefee,
wou'd be very extraordinary in this
Affair.

Affair. *Panaretus* he knew to be Pre-ingag'd, and therefore he immediately acquitted him of all Treachery in the Cafe : And being as we before obferv'd of a Soul, truely Noble, and Mafculine, he refolv'd, fince he found fhe had Thoughts of another, not to be Con-cern'd about her. But knowing *Pana-retus* to be of an Exalted and Generous Nature, he cou'd not difcharge himfelf from the Curiofity, of endeavouring to know how he wou'd Act in the Mat-ter. He therefore never gave *Panaretus* the leaft Intimations, of what he had obferv'd ; but perfwaded him two or three times to Accompany him in his Vifits to *Dorinda*, (which he continu'd as before) thereby getting repeated Confirmations of the reality, of what he had before obferv'd.

Whilft *Phylaftratus* had thus for a-bove a Month, taken Cognifance of the concern *Dorinda* was under, without her in the leaft fufpecting it ; fhe found the Effects of the Paffion fhe had con-ceiv'd for *Panaretus*, fo Raging, and

C Im-

Impetuous, as made her in Contempt of all the common Sentiments of her Sex: Refolve fome way or other to Communicate it to him. It is impoffible to exprefs the infin re Perplexity fhe was under, before fhe cou'd come to this Refolution. The Extravagancy of the Attempt appear'd to her, in fo many frightful Forms, that fhe knew not how to Face them. For her, who had fo often been fu'd to, even for the leaft favourable Afpect, by the moft exalted Young Gentlemen of the Age: Now her felf to Sue, this was terrible, beyond all Conception to her Soul! No Language can here defcribe the Convulfive Agonies of her Mind! But Affection having by repeated Strugles, violently bore down all Oppofition. At laft, with a Mind wholly, as it were given up to Defperation, and Regardlefs of what e're might be the Confequence, after fhe had Lock'd her felf up clofe in her Clofet, took her Pen, and gave vent to her Paffion in the following Lines.

Sir,

SIR,

BE *not surpriz'd, if the Repose I put in your* Generosity, *over rules the common Notions of my Sex: And makes me in Contempt both of them, and Custom, Let this Paper tell you, what I had much rather, you had perceiv'd your self, than I have been thus put to the Blush, in giving you such an unusual sort of Intelligence; but Necessity has no Law. The mighty Secret even forces it self to your Knowledge: And tho' happy* Phylaſtratus, *has his* Panaretus *to plead for him; yet Poor* Dorinda *muſt in ſpight of all Reluctance, alone plead for her ſelf. Pitty then not only my Paſſion, but peculiar Unhappineſs: Since I am not only forc'd to Love you, but tell you of it too my ſelf. I am perſwaded you are too Generous to* Triumph *over my Weakneſs, and hope your Candor will excuſe the daring Boldneſs of it. Fare you well; my Mind is under too great Diſtraction, to be formal in my Concluſion. I*

am

am (you muſt pardon my fondneſs) your real Admirer,

Dorinda.

It is altogether needleſs to Dilate here upon the various Difficulties, ſhe found in Compoſing this Billet, and many Sheets of Gilt-Paper ſhe ſpoil'd before ſhe had compleated it; Whether ſhe Wrote it at one, or many Sittings ; with abundance of other ſuch nice Impertinences. Omitting therefore all Scrutiny of this Nature ; we'll trace her in the ſucceeding part of her Conduct.

Having thus by Writing, a little diſcharg'd her Breaſt of that Load of Anxiety, with which ſhe before found her ſelf ſo ſenſibly Oppreſs'd : She began next to revolve in her Mind, how to Convey this Letter into *Panaretus's* Hands. If ſhe ſent it by the Penny-Poſt, ſhe run the Riſque of its coming into his Father's Hands, with whom he Liv'd ; to ſend it by her Maid, wou'd put her under a Neceſſity of letting her
into

into the Secret, and thereby Commencing her Equal. After fome confideration therefore, fhe refolv'd fome way or other fo to manage *Phylaftratus*, as to make him her Meffenger ; fo determin'd with her felf to take the firft opportunity that offer'd to effect it.

Phylaftratus renewing his Vifits to her, in his ufual Manner, and being eager to pufh Matters on to fome Iffue ; frequently (with all the feeming indifference in the World) made mention of *Panaretus*, taking a fecret Delight in Obferving the Viciffitudes of her Countenance, upon the leaft and moft indifferent Expreffions concerning him ; and always fo artfully contriving his Subject, as to fteal in the mention of him, in fuch a feeming accidental manner, as gave her not the leaft miftruft of his Defign. So far was fhe from having the leaft Hints of it, that fhe Conftru'd this Procedure to Adminifter a favourable Opportunity for her ; and therefore the next time he began to bring in fome Difcourfe about him:

She

She difplay'd an abundant readinefs to continue the Subject.

Phylaftratus, finding her in fuch a tangible Humour, foon made that Improvement of it, as at once Accomplifh'd both their defires; by affording them both an Opportunity mutually to Confumate the Plot, they had fo Induftrioufly Premeditated. The Difcourfe they were enter'd on, feem'd fo naturally Introductive, to what *Dorinda* defign'd; that fhe imagin'd Heaven it felf confpir'd to Facilitate her Contrivance; and the Gaiety of her Afpect, and Freedom of her Converfe, was fo very extraordinary thereupon, as gave *Phylaftratus* great Reafon to expect fome new Difcoveries. Things being thus, by an odd train of Accidents brought to this Crifis; and he Profecuting his Difcourfe about *Panaretus,* amongft many other Perfections, which he put him up as a great Mafter of, he particularly mention'd his Expertnefs at his Bufinefs. *Dorinda* having with abundance of Satisfaction, attended to what
fhe

she thought was purely an accidental
Panegyric, on her belov'd *Panaretus*:
Hearing him mention the Word Business, with abundance of Precipitance,
" Ask'd him, what his Business was?
Having as she imagin'd a very advan-
tageous Opportunity to Carry on her
Plot. *Phylastratus* finding by the flush
of her Face, and eagerness of Speak-
ing, she design'd to make some Improvements on the Word, so subtilly indulg'd her Inquiry, that he soon discover'd the very Bottom of her Intention. " His Business Madam, answer'd,
" he is a *Lawyer*; his Father is a Coun-
" cellour, and has brought him up with
" him to the same Calling. I believe
" I have some Affairs that lye in his
" Province : (reply'd *Dorinda,* altoge-
" ther unapprehensive, of his having the
" least Thoughts what those Affairs
" were) There are some Writings I
" have by me of my Fathers, which are
" likely to cause a Dispute between
" me, and some other Legatees : I
" wish *Panaretus* was to see them, be-

C 4   " cause

" cauſe he cou'd Adviſe me how to Act.
" Yes Madam, anſwer'd *Phylaſtratus,*
" no doubt on't; I'll tell him you want
" to ſpeak with him, if you pleaſe. No
" Sir, anſwer'd *Dorinda* (with a quick-
" neſs of Stratagem, for which, her
" Sex is noted.) Now I recollect a little,
" I remember the Words that Ad-
" miniſter the Matter for Conteſt, are
" very few; and ſince I have the Wri-
" tings by me in my Cloſet, I'll e'en
" Write the Words down which are
" Thought to bear a doubtful Senſe,
" and the Inferrences made from them;
" that ſo *Panaretus* may be better able
" to Judge of my Cauſe: And there-
" fore if you'll oblige me ſo far, as to
" carry me a Letter to him, I'll go im-
" mediately up into my Cloſet, and
" Write him my Caſe. *Phylaſtratus*
willing to appear, as great a Tool as
ſhe endeavour'd to make him, very
readily agreed to her Propoſal: Whereupon ſhe immediately Retir'd, and
added the following Poſtcript to her
Letter, *viz.*

" I

" *I have poſſeſs'd* Phylaſtratus, *that*
" *this comes about ſome Writings, in*
" *which your Calling is concern'd; I hope*
" *you'll have ſo great a Regard to my*
" *Credit, as to humour the Matter.*

Having wrote theſe Words, and Sealed
it up, She inſtantly deliver'd to *Phylaſtratus,* who promis'd punctually to
deliver it into *Panaretus's* Hands, the
firſt time he ſaw him ; and with a
ſeeming Innocence of Expreſſion, told
her, he'd take care to bring her *Panaretus's* Opinion of her Caſe, the next
time he came to give her a Viſit. Upon
which parting with her, he left her
infinitely pleas'd with the imaginary
Succeſs of her Project.

Phylaſtratus having thus artfully
gain'd *Dorinda's* Letter into his Hands,
was inflam'd with the utmoſt Curioſity,
to ſee it's Contents ; and having retir'd
for that Purpoſe, with a very little
Difficulty, got it open without any
Rent in the Paper, and it being Sealed
with a Wafer, was under no Concern
how to cloſe it up again, without any

Diſco.

Difcovery. Having then thus far effected his Defign with Succefs, and read the Letter over with abundance of fteady Attention : The Excefs of her Paffion, therein difclos'd, and moving Patheticnefs of her Language, at once attracted his Pitty and Admiration. It did indeed, at firft, a little regret him, to find what a Part fhe had allotted him ; but confidering the Violence of her Affection neceffitated her to it, he refolv'd, at leaft, to feem quietly to acquiefce in it ; and therefore fealing up the Letter, as he before found it, determin'd to carry it, as he had promis'd, to *Panaretus* : Concluding further, if *Panaretus* did not communicate the Bufinefs to him, he wou'd proceed gravely to tell his Story, as if he was really as much a Tool, as *Dorinda* had endeavour'd to make him.

Agreeable to this Refolution then he went to *Panaretus*, and gave him the Letter ; and with all imaginable Appearance of Innocence, told his Story, as *Dorinda* had laid it ; adding, that *Dorinda* defir'd

fir'd him to bring his Anfwer in Writing (this he faid, the better to get the
Sight of his Anfwer to her) the firft
Opportunity, in cafe he cou'd not come
to her to difcourfe about it. *Panaretus*
having heard his Story, and read *Dorinda*'s Letter, was ftruck with the utmoft Aftonifhment. The Surprize he
was under, render'd him incapable of
fpeaking a Word, without Hefitation.
Things appear'd to him, in every Circumftance, fo unaccountably extravagant, he cou'd not tell what to make
of them: But after fome Reflection,
finding the Language of her Letter too
piercing to be the Effect of any Trick;
and that fhe preffingly engag'd him in
it; to put a good Face on the Matter,
he fufpended his Surprize with as much
Artifice as he poffibly cou'd; and carry'd on the Story, agreeable to the
Scheme fhe had laid him.

Phylaftratus finding he endeavour'd
to blind the Matter, correfpondent to
his preceeding Determination; feem'd
to take all he faid, for granted, and
fwallow

ſwallow the Bait with all the Eaſe imaginable. He did not ſo much as break
a Jeſt upon him, but gravely deſir'd
him to direct *Dorinda* ſo to proceed, as
might give a quick Diſpatch to the
Broil ſhe was like to be engag'd in.

Panaretus ſeeing him (as he thought)
ſo finely gull'd, made him as grave Returns, promiſing he wou'd conſider
Dorinda's Caſe with the utmoſt Attention, and either write, or go himſelf,
and tell her his Opinion, very ſuddenly;
and ſo parted with him, for that Time.

Phylaſtratus being gone, he went
immediately to his Study, and again un-
folded *Dorinda*'s Letter, ſtrictly remarking every Particle of it; reading
it over and over, with the greateſt
Confuſion imaginable. He found himſelf, by it, encompaſs'd with ſuch a La-
byrinth of Difficulties, as run him almoſt to Diſtraction. *Phylaſtratus*, he
thought for his Part, wou'd take it he-
niouſly ill, to be thus betray'd of his
Miſtreſs. *Dorinda*, he fear'd, if ſhe
found her ſelf ſlighted, wou'd be deſ-
perate

perate: And yet, he found himself, on all Accounts, under an impoſſibility of making her any favourable Returns. Eſteem, reſpect, admire her he cou'd; but love her, Court her, that was not in his Power. His Soul was an utter Stranger to Falſhood; *Cælia*! *Cælia*! had gain'd the Precedence; ſhe was the Miſtreſs of his Vows, and the Affection that produc'd them, made them inviolably Sacred. He found himſelf attacqu'd on all Sides. The Wit, Beauty, and Affection of *Dorinda*, touch'd him with the tendereſt Senſe of Pitty; but his Faith to his Friend, his Miſtreſs, his *Cælia*! cou'd not, muſt not be ſuperceeded. To grieve *Dorinda*, he was loth, very loth; but to be perfidious to his Friend, falſe to his Vows, an Apoſtate to his Affection, he cou'd not bear. He was unacquainted with our modern Notion of Wit; Villany was no accompliſhment in his Eye; nor betraying the Fair, the Mark of a Gentleman. Goodneſs and Greatneſs, to him were *Synonimous Terms*, and he cou'd not
apprehend

apprehend how Veracity, which is one
of the bright Perfections of the Deity,
cou'd be thought a Blemiſh, when found
in his Image. In this Variety of Per-
plexities, he found it very Difficult to
determine with himſelf, how to proceed : At laſt, having weigh'd every
Circumſtance, with the moſt ſerious
Attention, he reſolv'd, ſteadily to ad-
here to his Faith, both to his Friend, and
Miſtreſs ; and yet, to uſe *Dorinda* with
that Tenderneſs and Reſpect, as ſhou'd
give her an evident Demonſtration, he
did not contemn, nor ſlight her Paſſion;
and thereupon took his Pen, and Wrote
to her, as follows, *viz.*

M A D A M,

Y*O.U deſire an Impoſſibility. Be not
ſurpriz'd ! impoſſible, beyond Expreſſion ; bid me invert the ſtated Courſe
of Nature ; diſcover all the ſecret Meanders, of Cauſes and their Effects ; or
(which wou'd yet advance my Labour to a
greater Toil) comprehend the vaſt Extent*
of

of your fhining Qualities. *Thefe wou'd
be meer Trifles, when oppos'd to fuch a Defire. No! Madam, my Vanity never yet
tower'd fo high. Had a Paper (carrying
in every Part fuch fubftantial Encomiums
on its Author) been the pleafing Entertainment of my Nocturnal Slumbers, per-
haps the Oddnefs of its Circumftances
might have been pafs'd by, with a few fuperficial Reflections of the fucceeding Day:
But when I had perfuaded my felf, that I
was really awake (which I cou'd not foon
do) my Mind was, it cou'd not be otherwife, but fill'd with the greateft Aftonifhment. I cou'd not imagine, that a Lady
of your exalted Endowments, plentiful Fortune, and celebrated Beauty, cou'd ever have
had any Regard to One, fo much below you:
But when I view your Letter, couch'd in
the Terms of Affection, you bear even to
me. Pardon me Madam, if the Confci-
oufnefs of my Want of Merit, makes me
again recommend my particular Friend,
and now your deluded Meffenger, Phylaftratus, as one whofe fublime Genius,
renders him alone, fit to poffefs fo vaft a
Bleffing;*

Blessing ; *whilst I take Pride in being ad-mitted into the Crowd of those, who esteem themselves happy, in serving you even in the meanest Offices : Or if my Reward must be commensurate to your generous Intentions towards me*, *permit me to subscribe my self your sincere Friend, and Admirer,*

Panaretus.

P. S.

I have taken all imaginable Care to manage your Plot, in Referrence to the deluded Phylastratus ; *tho' I must confess, if it had not been better founded by your Ingenuity, than any Conduct, in me, it had inevitably fail'd ; being really so amaz'd in perusing your Letter, that I cou'd scarce speak a rational Word. That we may then carry Matters on, as we have now begun them, I wou'd desire you to observe, that the Impression of my* Seal, *is a* Sun-Flower, *with this Motto over it,* Tibi Soli : *This I conceive, is a likely Means to put a Cheek to any Curiosity in* Phylastratus, *at least, will enable you to dis-*

cover

*cover whether he has open'd it, tho' I be-
lieve you need not fear it.*

Phylaſtratus, by his artful Expreſſions
of Readineſs, to carry his Anſwer, having anticipated all Concern in *Panaretus,*
how to convey this Letter into her
Hands, he immediately reſolv'd, without any Demur in the Matter, to give
it him the next time he ſaw him, to
carry it to her ; imagining *Dorinda* had
ſo well laid the Plot, as to leave no Room
for the leaſt Danger of Diſcovery.

Two or three Days having paſs'd,
ſince *Phylaſtratus* had given *Dorinda's*
Letter to *Panaretus*; he thought it high
time then to go to him, to ſee what Effect
it had wrote upon him. And accordingly ſetting his Countenance to a pitch
of Gravity, went to a *Tavern,* and ſent
for *Panaretus,* who immediately came
to him. Common Ceremonies having
paſs'd, and Both ſeated, *Phylaſtratus* told
him, " The Reaſon of his ſending for
" him then was, becauſe he was going
" to *Dorinda,* who, he ſuppos'd, wou'd
" enquire of him, about the Writings
                                    " ſhe

" she had sent to him ; and therefore
" desir'd him to inform him what An-
" swer to make her. *Panaretus* strictly remarking the Steadiness of his Countenance, Answer'd with abundance of
Freedom : " That he had fully weigh'd
" the Lady's Case, and had Wrote his
" Opinion concerning it ; and pulling
" the Letter out of his Pocket, added,
" That since he was going to her, he'd
" get him to carry it to her. *Phylastra-*
tus finding, what he earnestly desir'd
to see, as it were forc'd into his Hands;
very readily assented to his Proposal,
and taking the Letter from him, promis'd to give it her the next Day following; after which, having both of
them Drank *Dorinda* and *Calia's* Health,
they Parted.

Phylastratus, having with so little
difficulty got *Panaretus's* Letter into
his Possession, open'd it by heating the
Wax ; with the greatest Eagerness imaginable. The Perusal of it, so highly
endear'd his Friend *Panaretus* to him,
that he knew not how to forgive himself,

felf, of that feeming Act of Treachery,
in prefuming to open it. He difcover'd
fomething in it, fo generoufly tender
to *Dorinda*, and yet bore fuch a fublime Regard, to the Friendfhip between them, as render'd him unable to
defift Upbraiding himfelf, for fo much
as appearing to miftruft him. His
Mind indeed wholly acquitted him, of
having any bafe Defign towards either
Panaretus or *Dorinda,* but the Generous Faithfulnefs he found difplay'd
in the Letter; rais'd fuch a Noble
Emmulation in his Breaft, that he cou'd
not but think the Covertnefs of his
Procedure, carry'd the Marks of fomething Mean, and Abject in it. But
that which moft of all Affected him,
was the Precaution *Panaretus* had given
Dorinda, concerning his Seal. This
was a difficulty, he did not know how
to get over for a great while: Shou'd
it be Seal'd with any other Impreffion,
he readily forefaw, he fhou'd be Detected ; to get *Panaretus*'s Seal from
him, was altogether Impracticable :
The

The bare mention of it to him, being likely to raise his Jealousy. At last, he resolv'd to go to an *Engraver*, and get him to Cut him the same Device upon another Seal, as was on *Panaretus*'s: And thereupon, going to an Ingenious Artificer of that kind, soon gave him such a Description of it, as render'd him Capable of supplying him with such another.

Having by this Assistance, sufficiently furnish'd himself for the Concealment of his Plot; he quickly resum'd fresh Resolutions (notwithstanding his preceeding remorse) of looking into all the Letters that shou'd pass between them, if they came to his Hands; and using his little Imployment to make an Impression Posted to *Dorinda*'s with the Letter, with full purpose to use his utmost Endeavours to worm her out of another Letter, in Answer to it, by all possible Methods, that were Compatible to the Covertness of his Design.

Being thus Equip'd, and Resolv'd, he

he foon made fuch Advances in his
Steps, as brought him quickly to *Vul-*
pone's Door, and by one fingle wrap
gain'd Admittance, and a tedious Welcome from the Old Man; who was
fo full of his Congratulations, that
he cou'd not conceive where he wou'd
end. No fooner was he enter'd, but
he Saluted him with an, " Oh! *Phy-*
" *laftratus,* Matters goe rarely now;
" why there are fo many Various, Sun-
" dry, Divers, and Manifold Alterati-
" ons in my Neice of late, that 'twill
" make you ftare when you hear them.
" Ay! you are a Wagg, a very Wagg,
" I find; you know how to touch the
" Ladies in the right Part: For my
" part, I thought the Girl wou'd have
" run Mad with asking after you; I
" told you I'd do my uttermoft, and
" Addads! fhe begins to come to a-
" main. You fhan't be in her Com-
" pany now fcarcely Half an Hour;
" but prefently, fhe's wondring you
" han't been here; and if at any time
" fhe's been out any where, the firft
                              " Queftion

" Queſtion *Iſabella* is ask'd, is, whether
" *Phylaſtratus* has been here. The Old
Gentleman continu'd his Story in this
manner for a conſiderable Time : Taking
abundance of Pains to let *Phylaſtratus*
underſtand, that this Alteration in
Dorinda, was partly at leaſt effected, by
his over and above Care, and Induſtry,
the better to enhance the Price of his
Performances, and give him a ſort
of Intelligence of the Obligations he lay
under towards him.

Phylaſtratus eaſily gather'd, that
Dorinda's Carriage proceeded from another Cauſe, than what the Old Man
imagin'd : But being before reſolv'd to
make no diſcovery, and willing then
to humour the Comedy, he ſeem'd very
readily to concur with him in the Inferrences, he made from her Proceedings;
and ſo wittily ſooth'd him in his Miſtake, and extol'd his Conduct, that
he at once indulg'd his Pride, and made
himſelf Diverſion. But being in a little
time quite ſurfeited with his Impertinence, and deſirous himſelf to be a
Spectator

Spectator of *Dorinda's* Behaviour, he
desir'd him, to procure him her Company: Whereupon he inftantly order'd *Ifabella* to go and tell her *Phylaftratus* was there, and defir'd her
Prefence; and upon her Appearance,
gave them the agreeable Compliment
of his Abfence.

Being thus left alone together, *Dorinda's* impatience to hear what Effect
her Letter had, upon *Panaretus*,
foon gave *Phylaftratus* Occafion, to
give her his Letter, and proceed to tell
his Story. " I deliver'd your Paper,
" Madam, faid he, to *Panaretus*, who
" told me, next time I faw him after-
" wards, that upon the beft Judgment
" he cou'd form of your Cafe, by what
" you had wrote, he had fent his O-
" pinion in this Paper (giving her the
" Letter) and accordingly defir'd me to
" deliver it to you. *Dorinda* taking the
Letter, thank'd him for his Trouble,
" telling him fhe'd look over what he
" had fent very carefully ; and if fhe
" had happen'd any ways by her Hafte
when

" when she wrote last, to omit any
" Thing material, she'd take effectua
" Care to let him have a thorough In-
" formation of the whole Matter, by
" some Means or other, very shortly,
Phylastratus answer'd very gravely,
" he did not doubt his Friend *Panaretus*
" wou'd do his utmost to serve her, tell-
" ing her she might repose in him. *Do-*
rinda opening the Letter, and reading
it through,   as *Phylastratus* said this,
smil'd and said,   "I believe *Panaretus*
"and you,   have made a Bargain to
" praise one another.   Why Madam?
" reply'd *Phylastratus*, has he ever call'd
" me a Lawyer? A Lawyer! (said *Dorin-*
" *da*) why is that such a Mark of Com-
" mendation? If it be not a Mark of
" Commendation, you have made it a
" Mark of Happiness Madam, said
" *Phylastratus*.   Why so pray? Says
" *Dorinda*. Because *Panaretus*'s bearing
" that Name, render'd him capable of
" being serviceable to you Madam, an-
" swer'd he;   a Thing so desirable, I
" cou'd wish to be a Lawyer my self.

At this *Dorinda* blush'd, and look'd
on the Impreffion of the Wax of the
Letter, to fee if 'twas agreeable to
the Account *Panaretus* had given of it;
and finding it was, quitted her Diforder,
concluding what *Phylaftratus* had faid,
was purely accidental. *Phylaftratus* on
the other fide, obferving how his Drol-
lery had affected her, declin'd any further Profecution of it; and continu'd
the Converfation for about half an Hour
afterwards, with the common Gallan-
tries us'd to the Ladies; and then took
his Leave of her.

Dorinda having parted with *Phylaftratus*, retir'd to make a further Scrutiny
into her beloved *Panaretus*'s Letter, and
did not then content her felf, with only
a fuperficial View of it, but read it over
and over, with the moft intenfe Ap-
plication of Mind: Various were the
Thoughts fhe had of its Contents, and
as various the Refolutions fhe form'd
thereupon. That *Panaretus* declin'd
her Suit, fhe cou'd not but perceive,
but yet fo violent was her Paffion, and

D   fan-sanguine her Hopes, that she cou'd not, or rather wou'd not believe he contemn'd it. Infinite were the Perturbations of her Breast ; but because she did in her Answer to him, give a livelier Picture of them, than any other Hand, tho' never so artful, can possibly draw : We will omit any further Essays of that Kind, and present that more beautiful Description, which flow'd immediately, from her own Pen, that the Reader may have the most advantagious Idea of them.   Her Letter then to *Panaretus,* was as follows, *viz.*

Unkind, but yet Generous M A N.

HARD Fate ! Why ? Oh ! why must I thus engage, in a Task so uncommon, so unfit for my Sex ? Where will my Extravagances end ? Vain Creature that I am, why do I aspire so much above my Reach ? tempt my Fate, and proclaim my Folly ! I know, I have experienc'd indeed, you are too generous to disclose it ; and I must yet hope you will Pardon me, if I a-
                                              gain

gain venture boldly to plead a Cause, on which my Happiness, my Life depends: Urge me not therefore to look on Phyla-stratus, *or any Body but your self; no! it's true, my Heart is a foolish, a fond Heart, but it shall never be a Vagrant, a Prostitute; it is a Bankrupt I confess, but you are the sole Proprietor to it, it cannot, it won't admit a Dividend. I have not so little Notion of Merit neither, to think it e'er the less, because 'tis disclaim'd by its happy Possessor: And therefore that modest Defference, you so nobly pay to others, has been so far from loosing, that it has faster riveted my Chains: But I strive to reconcile Antipathies, I am not worthy of* Panaretus, *and therefore, must remain the Disconsolate, the Distressed*

Dorinda.

The Excess of her Passion so blinded her Judgment, that she had now no manner of Concern, how to convey this into *Panaretus*'s Hands. *Phylastra-tus,* she imagin'd, was so effectually

impos'd

impos'd on, that there was no Danger of his making any Difcovery; fhe thought fhe had fufficiently anticipated all Difficulty of that kind, by the Curfory Mention fhe made to *Phyla-ftratus*, of looking again over the Writ-ings, to fee whether fhe had given *Pa-naretus* a juft Account of her Cafe; and therefore concluded, it was but telling *Phylaftratus* fhe had made fome lit-tle Miftake in her Tranfcription; and adding fome Stratagem, the bet-ter to introduce it, and all her Work of that Nature wou'd be accomp-lifh'd.

As fhe was thus entertaining her Fancy with the pleafing Delufion, *Vul-pone* having not been alone with her, fince her laft Interview with *Phylaftratus*: And being Curious to know what Effect it had upon her; becaufe fhe had fo often exprefs'd fuch an unufual Defire to fee him, before he came; rufh'd in upon her, and finding her in a thought-ful Pofture; with a chearful Afpect ac-cofted her, as follows. "So Neice!
you

" you 're very ſtudiouſly bent : I'el war-
" rant you 're thinking of *Phylaſtratus*
" now ; but I can't blame you, for he's
" really a very pretty Young Gentle-
" man as ever I knew ; he does deſerve
" the beſt of your Thoughts ; he is not
" one of the Vap'ring, huffing Blades of
" the Town, no ! he is a Man of Sub-
" ſtance, Girl ; 'sbud ! as far as I can
" underſtand, he deſigns to have a
" Charriot on purpoſe for you ; and
" then you'll have ſuch a Retinue,----
" well I ſwear he's a ſweet Gentleman.
The Old Gentleman wou'd have gone
on to the end of the Chapter, with this
ſort of Rapſody ; but *Dorinda* quite impatient to find her Thoughts ſo wretch-
edly inverted, interrupting him, ſaid,
" far be it from me to detract from either
" his Qualifications or Fortune ; and
" therefore, as I am not conſcious of
" having ſo much Vanity ; neither can
" I eaſily perſuade my ſelf he has ſo little
" Judgment, as to beſtow his Charriot, or
" any other ſuch large Inſtances of his
" Favour, on ſuch an undeſerving Ob-
                                    " ject.

" ject. I am not so unacquainted with
" the World, as not to know the Mo-
" tives generally influence such young
" Gentlemen as *Phylaſtratus*: They take
" a Delight to sooth the natural Vanity,
" and Levity of my Sex, and think
" they can no ways render their Com-
" pany grateful to us, without seeming
" as extravagantly to admire us, as we
" do our selves: I have heard them,
" when they have been in an ingenuous
" Mood, frankly acknowledge, that
" the Reason why they think them-
" selves oblig'd to addreſs themselves to
" the Ladies, with such a Heap of re-
" dundant Compliments; is, because,
" they think by that time we are ar-
" riv'd to Fifteen, we are so thoroughly
" acquainted with the repeated Exer-
" ciſe of our Glaſs; and consequently,
" are poſseſs'd with such a weak Fond-
" neſs of our own Pretty Faces, that
" when ever we converse with them,
" and they don't make our personal Per-
" fections the sole Subject of their Dis-
" course, we imagine them highly In-
" jurious

"jurious to us. Whether the Gene-
"rality of my Sex's Conduct will vin-
"dicate the Justice of this Assertion, I
"will not now dispute; but this I re-
"solve, my Proceedings shall ne'er be
"an Illustration of it; it shall ne'er be
"said, that *Dorinda* courted Praise;
"or when she had it, was elated by it.
"No! I like *Phylastratus*'s Galantry well
"enough; but yet I am not so vain,
"as not to guess at the Intention of it.

Vulpone going to reply, was interrupted by a sudden Knocking at the Door,
and *Isabella* being not immediately present, went himself and open'd it. Upon which, he found himself saluted by
Phylastratus.

Vulpone seeing him, instantly receiv'd him in, and huddl'd him with
great Haste into a back Room, where
he began immediately to dinn his Ears
with what had pass'd between him
and his Neice, just before he came,
telling him he'd left her alone in her
Room, to come to let him in, prompt-

ing

ing him further to go and surprize her. *Phylaſtratus* coming on purpoſe to hear what Effect *Panaretus's* Letter had had upon *Dorinda,* very readily comply'd to what was propos'd ; and accordingly trip'd ſoftly up Stairs, the better to come on her unexpectedly. In the Interim *Dorinda* (being by *Phylaſtratus's* knocking at the Door, deliver'd from the ungrateful Perſecution of her Unkle's Converſation)   again   reſum'd the Thoughts of managing her Plot, in Reference to the Conveying her Letter to *Panaretus* ; and thinking her ſelf ſufficiently ſecur'd, from any further Interruption by her Unkle, proceeded to add the following Poſtſcript to her Letter, *viz.*

" *I thank you very kindly, for the Care* " *you have taken to be ſecret.   I found* " *the Impreſſion of your Seal, as you de-* " *ſcrib'd it ; and therefore don't queſtion* " *ſo to manage* Phylaſtratus, *as to make* " *him again my deluded Meſſenger, as you* " *call him.*

As ſhe was writing, *Phylaſtratus* made

made his Appearance, at which, with
a quickneſs of Thought, diſſembling
the Surprize ſhe was under (after he
made a previous Apology, for his Intruſion ſo ſuddenly) ſhe told him, "ſhe
" was then writing to *Panaretus,* and
" ſince he was come ſo opportunely, ſhe
" ſhou'd take it as a Favour, if he'd be
" ſo kind to carry her Letter to him.
" For added ſhe, upon a Scrutiny into
" *Panaretus*'s Letter, finding I had made
" ſome ſmall Miſtakes, in the Account
" I had given him. I have rectify'd
" them now, and ſo ſuppoſe there will
" be no further Occaſion of giving either
" you, or *Panaretus,* any more Trou-
" ble.— I am ſo far, anſwer'd *Phyla-*
" *ſtratus,* from eſteeming what you
" deſire any Trouble, that I take it ts
" be a great Addition to my Happineſs,
" to be capable of being any ways ſer-
" viceable to you.— They continu'd
this Interview for about half an Hour
with abundance of trifling Ceremonie
of the ſame Nature: After whien

Phy

Phylaftratus, taking the Letter, parted with her.

After he was gone, *Dorinda* exceedingly delighted her felf with the thoughts
of her Management, in turning his
accidental Surprizing of her, fo effectually to be a Means of conveying her
Letter into *Panaretus*'s Hands. The De-
duction fhe made, feem'd fo very natural, and free from being any ways
ftrain'd, that fhe thought it impoffible
Phylaftratus fhou'd have any Miftruft.
On the other fide, *Phylaftratus,* having
thus before he expected, got *Dorinda*'s
Letter into his Poffeffion, having at once
perus'd it, and admir'd it, feal'd it up
again, and went immediately with it
to *Panaretus,* and deliver'd it to him.

Panaretus having receiv'd *Dorinda*'s
Letter, and given a melancholly Attention to *Phylaftratus*'s Story; with a
diffembl'd Air of Brisknefs told him,
" he wou'd carefully weigh *Dorinda*'s
" Cafe, and give her his Thoughts
" of it, as foon poffibly he cou'd:
And then, with an extorted chearful

ful Complacency, took his leave of him.

Being parted from him, and having thoroughly examin'd *Dorinda*'s Letter, he retir'd, to give it a full Consideration. As to his Resolution, he found That, not very difficult to make; but how to express it to *Dorinda* afforded him abundant Matter for Study : Tho' he was unalterably fixt to keep his Faith inviolably sacred ; and even, *Dorinda* shou'd not tempt him to break it ; yet, he cou'd not be insensible of the exalted Generousity of her Passion. He knew very well, that as his own Fortune was no ways Commensurate with her's ; neither was her's with *Phylastratus*'s ; and therefore he cou'd not but observe the Preference she had given him, was abstracted from all Thoughts of Gain, or rather a free Choice of the most disadvantageous Loss. As he was firmly determin'd not to be justly charg'd with Falshood by *Celia* : So he cou'd not be reconcil'd with being found guilty of Ingratitude to *Dorinda.* In fine, after he had labouriously canvass'd, the seve

ral

ral Circumftances of his Affairs, for a confiderable time, he disburden'd his Mind,
in the following Letter to *Dorinda,*

MADAM,

*T*HE *Irrefiftablenefs of your Charms,
even only in their exterior View, is
what you have often had fo large an Experience of; that but barely to mention them,
as fuch, wou'd but be an infipid Recital,
of what all that have ever had the Happinefs of feeing you, loudly proclaim.
But when (as I have done) we take a larger
flight of Contemplation, and maze our
felves with the dazling Beauties of your
Mind; when I fay we then gaze on all the
bright Imbellifhments of that Soul which
gives you a juft Title to the Name of* Phœ-
nix. *We are tempted to think you more
than Humane, and are ready to addrefs
you as fuch. I speak in Plural Number,
becaufe this is the concurrent Notion which
all that know you, have conceiv'd of you.
You can't then imagine, that I am the only
Perfon, fo ftupid as not to be fenfible, deeply*

ly *sensible,* of the exalted *Nature* of *your
Perfections.* No! *Madam,* I *am,* and
ever *will,* be *ready to pay the* greatest *Defference to them* ; *and if any Action that is
not dedicated to the Source of Beings,* may
be *lawfully* call'd *Adoration* ; 'tis *you,* 'tis
you *alone,* shou'd *receive the* distinguishing
Homage from me. Let *me intreat* you
then, *not to impute my declining your Request,* to *any indifferent or* slighting
Thoughts of your Merits ; *but a* greatful
Regard for your Tranquillity : *For my very
Soul* shudders *at the Thoughts of that
Trouble, which the Prosecution of an A-
mour, with* such *an incompatiable Object,
will* necessarily *involve you in.* You *can't
be* insensible, *Madam* (*how favourable* soever *the Opinion you have* conceiv'd *of me
may be*) *that your* Unkle *will be* strangely
averse, to *your Burying your bright
Qualities, in the Arms of One, who* must
confess (*even in* spight *of the Vanity you
have tempted him to*) *he is* not *worthy of* so
immense a Blessing : *Therefore if I per-
suade you to transfer your Heart to One,
whose Merits lay a* juster *Claim to it,* by
all

all that's Lovely and Dear, let me conjure you to take it (as it really is defign'd) in pure Zeal, grateful Zeal, for the Prevention of your Unhappiness. Take this Madam, as the fincere Advice of One who loves you; loves you with a Flame more rais'd than ever Cupid *kindl'd; loves you with the Ardor of Angels, abftracted from all the grofs Ideas of Senfe; and will ever be ready (if poffible) with a Zeal ad-equal to thofe glorious Beings, to promote your Happinefs. Thefe are the undiffembled Sentiments of your fincere Friend, and Humble Servant,*

Panaretus.

P. S.

Finding Phylaftratus *fo well manag'd by your Ingenuity, I think I may ftill, without any Danger, continue to make him your deluded Meffenger.*

Panaretus having thus deliver'd his Mind, and being poffefs'd with the greateft Security of *Phylaftratus*'s being thoroughly impos'd on by *Dorinda,* found very little Difficulty in conveying

it

it to his Hands, and thereby (as he thought) gaining a fatisfactory Affu- rance of *Dorinda's* feeing it, without the leaft Interruption.

Phylaftratus being thus poffefs'd of *Panaretus's* Letter, and having perus'd it after his ufual Manner, found himfelf differently imprefs'd with it, than what he was by any of the former. The gene- rous Conftancy of *Panaretus* to *Calia*, appear'd to him fo extremely fublime, and unparallel'd ; that he cou'd not but entertain fome Thoughts that fhe did not merit it. The Temptation *Dorinda* gave him, was in its every Part fo par- ticularly moving, that his fo repeatedly declining her Suit, feem'd to him no lefs than a Miracle of Refolution : For as *Dorinda's* Fortune was abundantly fu- perior (or rather *Calia* had none at all) fo her Wit, her Education, her every Thing was fo immenfely rais'd a- bove *Calia's*, that they wou'd not admit the leaft Comparifon. *Calia* was a mean, ord'nary Girl, very little rais'd in her Character, above a common Servant:

vant: *Dorinda,* a Lady of the moſt po-
liſh'd Endowments, imbelliſh'd with all
the Beauties that a plentiful Fortune,
and liberal Education cou'd furniſh her
with ; and indeed, when *Cælia* was oppos'd to her, ſhe ſeem'd only as a Foil
to ſet her off with the greater Luſtre:
So far was ſhe in the Eye of *Phylaſtratus,*
from bearing any juſt Preference to her.

But finding all her alluring Rhetoric
unable to ſhock *Panaretus's* Affection, and having, as 'twere ſoliloqui'd
upon the ſeveral extraordinary Parts of
his Amour ; the peculiar Nobleneſs of
Nature *Panaretus* had diſplay'd, rais'd
ſuch enlarg'd Emulation in his Breaſt,
as render'd him altogether unable to forbear acting ſome conſiderable Part himſelf. *Panaretus* he thought, was too
generous to be deceiv'd, and ſhou'd he
not do his utmoſt, to prevent any thing
of that Kind ; he thought he cou'd not
acquit himſelf, of an ungrateful Negli-
gence towards him. Shou'd *Cælia* prove
falſe to him in the End, notwithſtand-
ing all that inviolable Affection, even
under

under the greateſt Temptation he bore
to her; he thought he ſhou'd not be a
Friend, at leaſt not a Friend worthy
of *Panaretus*, if he did make ſuch previous Diſcoveries of her curſs'd Inconſtancy, as might render him capable
of giving him timely Notice of it.
Beſides, he cou'd not but think (if
Cælia did not return his Affection with
a more than common Flame) that
Dorinda's Paſſion claim'd ſome, if
not a greater Regard. He cou'd not
but pitty her Misfortune; nor without
offering Violence to his own Breaſt, not
entertain ſome Thoughts of being help-
ful to her.

All his former ſecret Regret at her
giving *Panaretus* ſo large a Preference,
was now wholly abandon'd by him, and
all his Thoughts center'd in one continu'd Deſire of being aſſiſtant to her, in
procuring that Happineſs ſhe ſo earneſtly Coveted. And therefore he ſoon
commenc'd a Reſolution, of uſing all
poſſible Arts to diſcover *Cælia*'s Sincerity; determining further, if he detected
any

any thing of Falſhood in her, he'd make it at once, a Means to diſuade *Panaretus* from her, and thereby make *Dorinda's* Bliſs conſumate.

Having thus deliberated how to proceed, he went to *Dorinda,* and gave her *Panaretus's* Letter, leaving her, after a ſhort Converſe, to retire and make her own Reflections upon it.

His particular Intimacy with *Panaretus,* had made him long before very well known by *Celia*; and therefore how to get Acceſs to her was no Difficulty and the many great Advantages he had of him in Fortune, he thought wou'd be ſome Temptation to her. Being then ſo far qualify'd, he frequently came into *Celia's* Company, as frequently uſing all the little Dalliances that are common to Youth, towards her; often giving her large Harangues of the Irreſiſtableneſs of her Charms, omitting no Extravagances that all his Wit, and Fancy cou'd furniſh him with, to raiſe her Vanity, and Exerciſe her Levity and Inconſtancy.

Celia

Cælia finding her self caress'd by *Phylastratus*, with so much splendid Pageantry; and being before by *Panaretus*'s Choice of her, abundantly elated with the Thoughts of her own Perfections, very readily concluded, his so extraordinary Behaviour towards her, was the Effect of real and sincere Affection; and by the Help of her Glass, and indulgent Opinion of her self, so fully confirm'd this Thought, that she had not the least Doubt in the World concerning it. The possibility of his being set to Work by *Panaretus*: The Probability of what he did, being design'd only to try her, or at least make himself Diversion; the near similitude mere Complements, and real Affection bear to each other, and the Commonness of young Gentlemen, using Extravagances of that Kind, in the Ladies Company. These were Things she never thought on. No, the Greatness of his Fortune, the Magnificence of his Appearance, and the many other shining Advantages, he was Master of, so wholly engross'd her Thoughts.

Thoughts, and convey'd so many daz'l-
ing Ideas to her Imagination, as gave no
Room for any other Thoughts of *Panaretus*, or any thing else than such as were
the Effect of Resolution to justle Him
off.   It's true, *Panaretus* was once
thought a Prize; and no Arts, no Pro-
testation, no Vows were omitted to se-
cure him;   Heaven and Earth were
made Witnesses of her protested sincerity of Affection; and every Word she
spoke when that was the Subject, was
back'd with a peculiar Vehemency of
Asseveration;   but now, as oppos'd to
Phylastratus, he appear'd contemptible,
and no ways worth her Concern, and
she resolv'd for the future to treat him
as such.   Her Thoughts were wholly
taken up with her imaginary new Spark,
and all her preceeding Engagements to
Panaretus, as much so forgotten, as they
were deceitfully made.   *Phylastratus*
had Occasion to use very little Art to
make his Discoveries;   he needed not
pull her, she'd fall her self, into his Arms.
so soon was *Panaretus* forsaken by her,

fo light, fo inconftant was her Nature.

Phylaftratus obferv'd, the innate Levity of her Nature, with a Breaft inflam'd with the higheft Difdain; but being willing to trace her Falfhood; yet further, he conceal'd his Refentments, and proceeded on, to footh her in it as before. But determin'd for the future to be, rather Paffive, than Active; rather to hear what fhe wou'd fay, than fay any thing himfelf. However, he repeated his Vifits to her, as before; and took a very exact Account of her Carriage.

Cælia on the other fide, being mightily flufh'd with *Phylaftratus*'s Proceedings, immediately communicated the whole Matter to *Demigoga* her Mother, and *Sycophanta* her Sifter, and quickly in concert with them, agreed to fhove *Panaretus* off, the better to receive him. The Superiority of *Phylaftratus*'s Fortune, to that of *Panaretus*, fo effectually dazil'd their Underftandings, and ftifl'd their Confciences, that it gave no Room for the leaft Reflection of

either

either. *Panaretus* was grown fo Contemptible all on a fudden, that even the
Methods of turning him off, were not
worth a Thought: It was indeed a-
greed, that *Cælia* fhou'd abfent her felf
from him; but the Reafons upon which
She was, at leaft pretendedly to proceed, afforded them no manner of Study.
In fhort, the Gentleman fo fully out-
weigh'd the *Lawyer* and his Eftate, fo
abundantly Compenfated for all *Cælia*'s
preceeding Ingagements: That the ob-
taining of them, was thought fufficient to Cancel all other Obligations.

. Whilft thefe things pafs'd between
Phylaftratus and *Cælia, Dorinda* was fully
imploy'd in Canvafing *Panaretus*'s Letter. She found her felf at an infinite
Lofs what Conftruction to put upon
it. The Perplex'dnefs of its Com-
pofure, made it appear with an unaccountable Ambiguity unto her. His
Expreffions of a real Efteem towards
her, were fo very full and Pathetic,
that She cou'd not believe them feign'd,
and tho' indeed at prefent, he profefs'd,

to love her with the Ardour of Angels;
yet Time she hop'd wou'd convert it,
into that of a Gentleman. Various were
her Endeavours to account for his defiring her to transfer her Heart from
him, and as various the Difficulties she
found in the Attempt; but having, by
a continu'd Tract of Thought, run
over all that she cou'd possibly think
to be the true Reason of it, at last she
concluded it must necessarily be the Effect of some Ladies, being before hand
with her, and the Violence of her Affection had render'd her Judgment so unusu-
ally partial, that she cou'd not think it a
Crime to trick her (as she thought) happy Rival out of her Spark. This however,
she resolv'd, to use the utmost Stratagem
to gain Intelligence, whether he was
ingag'd to any other Lady, or no; and
she further determin'd with her self, that
none cou'd be a more effectual Me-
thod of doing this, than asking him to
write his Sentiments of the Passion of
Love. A Subject of this Nature, she
thought wou'd sufficiently put him to
the

the Teſt; and if he was any ways nearly concern'd in it, ſhe fully aſſur'd her ſelf he wou'd diſcover it by ſome of his Expreſſions. Beſides, to carry on the Encounter further with her Pen, ſhe found her ſelf altogether unable; and therefore as ſhe cou'd not gain her End, by open Force; ſhe found her ſelf under a Neceſſity of having Recourſe to Policy. She reſolv'd therefore to try this Project, and upon her gaining any Information thereby, to make ſuch Improvements as the Circumſtances of Things wou'd naturally admit of.

Panaretus, altogether inſenſible either of *Phylaſtratus's* Policy, or *Cælia's* Ingratitude, and having receiv'd no Reply from *Dorinda,* to his laſt Letter, concluded ſhe took it for her final Anſwer: And now deſign'd to deſiſt any further Procedure; and with this deluſive Opinion of his Affairs, proceeded to pay his Viſits to *Cælia,* in his wonted manner. The Place where he generally us'd to ſolace himſelf with her, being commonly her Siſter *Sycophanta's* Houſe;

House, he reforted there, in his accuftom'd manner, to meet her ; but
to his great Surprize, found his repeated
Endeavours to fee her, altogether Fruitlefs, and Unfuccefsful.

This Alteration prefently led him to
inquire what was the Reafon (of *Sycophanta*) that her Sifter abfented her felf
from him, who prefently anfwer'd with
an Air of Contempt, and Indifference,
" that *Demogoga*, her Mother, had
" taken fome fecret Difpleafure at him ;
" and therefore was refolv'd, that *Cæ-*
" *lia* fhou'd continue no longer to hold
" any Correfpondence with him. She
proceeded further, to give *Panaretus* all
the furly Treatment, that Want of
Senfe, and the Defire of turning him
off, to make Room for *Phylaftratus*,
joyn'd with the inbred Sordidnefs of
her Nature, cou'd fuggeft to her.
This unmannerly, as well as unexpected
Carriage of *Sycophanta*, ftruck *Panaretus*
to the Heart ; it rouz'd the higheft E-
motions of Anger, and Difdain in his
Breaft ; but fo tender was his Affection

E   to

to *Cælia*, and so hard was it for him, to construe any thing against her, that he wholly acquitted her; he cou'd not bear the Thoughts of her being culpable of any thing like Falshood. That *Demogoga*, and *Sycophanta*, were deceitful, sordid, and all that's base and abject, he cou'd easily believe; but that *Cælia* was any thing short of the brightest Innocence, he cou'd not entertain the Thought. He imagin'd she was as much afflicted by their so long Absence, as he; and so indulgent was the Regard he had to her, that he was more sensibly touch'd, with what he imagin'd she suffer'd, than with all that Load of Injuries which had been thrown on himself. Infinite were the Inquietudes, this alone Thought rais'd in his Breast, the Contempt, the Scorn, with which *Sycophanta* treated him, regretted him nothing, in comparison with the convulsive Agonies; with the Thoughts of *Cælia*'s being torn from his Arms against her will, caus'd in his Soul. His Fancy hitherto was very active,

tive, prefented a thoufand hideous
Forms of things to his Mind ; *Cælia* was
drefs'd up, by his teeming Imagination, as under the moft perplexing Doubts
of Mind ; affaulted with all the repeated Clamours, of a bufy and detracting
Malice ; and nothing that cou'd either
exagerate the accute Senfe he had of his
Misfortune, or confirm him in the
Thoughts of *Cælia*'s being equally op·
prefs'd by it, was pafs'd by, without
the moft cruciating, and tormenting
Reflections. He fancy'd he faw *Cælia*, befet with all that Malice, and
Ill-nature cou'd fuggeft ; tempted
with innumerable Infinuations, both
by *Demogoga*, and *Sycophanta*, to believe him falfe to her, and under the
moft wracking, and pungent Defpair
at the News. In fine, he joyn'd a fort
of Mad-man to the Lover, and made
(pardon the Odnefs of the Expreffion)
as ingenious a Fool as ever you faw in
your Life. And thus at prefent, our
Story requires us to leave him. the bet-

ter to trace the Proceedings of his Friend.

Phylastratus having abundantly detected the Perfidiousness of *Cælia,* took an Opportunity again to pay a Visit to *Dorinda,* who receiv'd him with a Brisknefs of Afpect, of late fomething unufual to her. After he was fet down, and fome trifling Preliminaries had pafs'd; fhe told him, "She was ex-
"ceedingly oblig'd to his Friend *Panare-*
"*tus,* for the great Trouble fhe had
"put him to; adding, that fhe believ'd
"now fhe fhou'd have no further Occa-
"fion to divert him from his more ne-
"ceffary Affairs, having now, fhe
"hop'd, fully accommodated all Diffe-
"rences. *Phylastratus* ftrictly obferving thefe Words of *Dorinda,* and thinking fhe had taken *Panaretus*'s laft Letter, as a final Denial; concluded, fhe now defign'd wholly to defift any further Profecution of her Suit, and was refolv'd to concern her felf no more about him. Here 'twas that all his Powers were, as 'twere, upon their full Stretch; a Thoufand

fand feveral Paffions revell'd in his Soul:
Here 'twas his Friendfhip to *Panaretus*
evidenc'd it felf in its brighteft Luftre;
infpir'd him with Thoughts too big for
Language to exprefs. That *Panaretus*,
after all his Faithfulnefs, fhou'd be a-
bandon'd, both by *Cælia*, and *Dorinda*
too; was a perfect Goad to his Soul.
No! he refolv'd it muft not, fhou'd not
be. He continu'd therefore the Difcourfe
about him to *Dorinda*, omitting nothing
he thought cou'd poffibly contribute to
re-kindle her Flame, and excite her
Paffion afrefh towards him; and a-
mongft many other things, having
mention'd fome facetious Lines of *Pana-*
retus's making, upon a waggifh Affair,
that they were both engag'd in: *Dorin-*
da interrupting him, faid, " I find then
" your Friend *Panaretus* is a Proficient
" in Poetry; I wifh I had known that be-
" fore, I wou'd have fet him a Task, for I
" love Poetry dearly.--- 'Tis not too late
" now, Madam, anfwer'd *Phylaftratus*.
Upon which feeming to decline with
an Air as gave ftrong Indications, that
the

she wanted to be press'd, to propose what she desir'd: *Phylastratus* taking the Hint, told her, " she must set *Pa-* " *naretus* a Task. To which seeming to comply with abundance of Reluctancy ; after a long Contest 'twas agreed by them both, that *Panaretus* shou'd write a Poem upon Love. Having gain'd thus far upon her, he earnestly importun'd her to write a little Note, to request him to do it ; pretending he was sure *Panaretus* wou'd not do it upon his Desire, having so often troubl'd him in that Nature before ; and by abundance of Intreaty persuaded her to do it. And thereupon (being mightily pleas'd to find her self, as 'twere forc'd to prosecute what she had long before projected) leaving *Phylastratus* alone, she retir'd into her Closet, and wrote to *Panaretus,* as follows, *viz.*

SIR,

BEING *inform'd by* Phylastratus, *your Friend, that your Skill in Num-*
bers

hers comes up to your other great Perfecti-
ons: I find my self prevail'd on, by his
Importunity, and my own Inclinations, to
request your Thoughts of that Kind, on the
Passion of Love.

Your Humble Servant,
to Command,

Dorinda.

Having wrote this, she instantly return'd to *Phylastratus*, and giving it to
him, earnestly charg'd him to use his
utmost Endeavours, to make *Panaretus*
comply with the Contents of it; in-
treating him further, as soon as ever he
had perform'd it to bring it to her.
Phylastratus promis'd to be punctually
observant of her Desire; and having
given her a full Satisfaction by his repeated Assurances, and himself much
Delight in so fully discovering her Stra-
tagems, he parted with her for that
Time.

Being thus possess'd of *Dorinda's* Letter, and having examin'd the Contents

E 4   of

of it, in his wonted manner, he posted
away with it to *Panaretus*, resolving to
admit of no Excuse for his Non-perfor-
mance of what it requir'd ; and having
sent for him to a Tavern where they
usually met, and deliver'd it to him,
soon made him to understand, that
neither *Dorinda*, nor he, wou'd take
any Denial.

Panaretus being in the utmost Confusion at the many perplexing Circumstances of his Affairs, began in the most
moving Expressions of an Intense Passion, to acquaint *Phylastratus* with the
whole Story of *Calia*'s Absence from
him ; inveighing with the most eager
Resentments, against the savage Ill nature of *Demogoga*, and *Sycophanta*, towards him ; and wholly acquitting
Calia from all guilt in the Matter. *Phylastratus*, tho' fully sensible of his Mi-
stake, thought fit for the Present to
dissemble his having Knowledge of
the Matter ; and having commiserated
his Misfortunes, and promis'd his
utmost Assistance to extricate him,
                                    still

ftill proceeding to prefs him to anfwer
Dorinda's Requeft, 'till having quite
wearied him out with his Importunity,
he promis'd (after having long urg'd the
Indifpofition he was under) to do it; after
which having drank a Glafs, or two, to
their better Succefs in their Amours for
the future, they took their Leaves.

Soon after their Parting, *Panaretus*
retir'd into his Study, and having largely revolv'd on the feveral unhappy Circumftances of his Amour, determin'd
with himfelf, at once to gratify *Dorinda's*
Requeft, and if poffible, ftill the many
Perturbations of his own Breaft, by the
following Lines, *viz.*

Love a PASTORAL.

Theocles.

WHO! my PHYLANDER? *Why fo penfive grown?*
What! folded Arms? Come now we are alike

Say from what Cause, proceeds this solid Grief,

A Vent of Sorrow is a sure Relief.

Why shunn'st thou so, the Pleasures other Swains,

Seek and enjoy, amidst their Happy Plains;

PHYLANDER speak, 'twill ease thy Misery,

Let me bear Part, at least, bear Sympathy.

Phylander.

Oh! THEOCLES————

Fly, Fly! the Influence of the Fair,

Those Banes of Peace, those Nurseries of Care.

Once! ————

(Oh! dire reverse of Things) once was I Bless

With all the Pleasures of an quiet Breast;

Calm Joy, and sweet Serenity of Mind,

I then, in ev'ry Verge of Life did find:

No raging Lust, of Pow'r no turns of State

Or Fortunes erring Wheel did Cares create,

To be content, I thought was to be Great;

I Shun'd the Revels, of Luxuriant Swains,

And 'scap'd their Crimes, as well as after Pains,

Each

Each Day regal'd me, with some fresh Delight,
And sweet Repose bless'd each revolving Night.
Sprightly I trip'd it o'er the Verdant Mead,
And took Delight my bleating Charge to feed;
With eager Zeal did nightly Vigils hold,
Hugging my Lambs, as Misers do their Gold;
Nicely observ'd their youthful Innocence,
And oft did Moral Lessons draw from thence;
Upon some Mossey Bank my self I'd lay,
And smile to see how chearfully they'd play;
Their little Pranks, still fresh Amusements brought,
And gave me Pleasure, 'bove the Reach of Thought.
Riches I spurn'd, my Mass of Treasure was
The little Vegetives, amid' the Grass;
Each minute Daisy, and fragrant Violet,
I valu'd more, than Diadems beset
With all the costly Jems of East and West,
And shinning Ore, by all, so much carest:
More Beauteous they appear'd unto my Sight,
And gave my Soul more sure, and real Delight.

Power I had, my Subjects did Obey,
My Crook to me, was as a Scepter's Sway;

No restless Subjects did disturb my Reign,
They knew not they, but I was Sovereign,
Never put Cases, when they might Rebel,
But strove which sheu'd in Loyalty excel :
Jointly conspir'd that I shou'd happy be,
And own'd my Power was from the Leity.

With purling Brooks my Pastures round were strow'd,
And numerous Shoals of Fishes in them flow'd ;
The spreading Willows, Shelter did afford,
And soft MEANDERS own'd me for their Lord ;
Each needful Blessing all kind Heav'n bestow'd.
I wanted nothing that was truly good.'

Thus was I bless'd, thus slid my Hours away,
'Till Woman, Beauteous Woman did betray
My Soul, which knew not her resistless Power
'Till Time had usher'd in that fatal Hour ;
In which from Cælia's Eyes, there flew a Dart,
That made an easy Victim, of my Heart ;.
From thence (curs'd Æra!) do I date those Pains,
That make me now the wretchedest of Swains ;

But *she appear'd so dazz' ing to my sight,*
Something methoughts I saw so heav'nly bright,
My Heart, by Violence, proclaim'd its self her right.

  Have you not seen, upon a dewy Morn,
What beauteous Lustre does the Rose adorn,
And how immaculate the Lillies are,
How snowy white, how glorious they appear?
These in her Face their liveliest Beauties mix'd,
And bless'd the fair Abode wherein they'd fix'd
Oh! She was heav'nly Fair in ev'ry Part,
A Miracle of Nature's labour'd Art.

  Fondly I gaz'd, and fir'd my Soul with Love,
Striving, in vain, the growing Pangs to brave,
I found each Nerve, some pungent Pain did prove,
My Struggle made me only more a Slave.
So the stout Beast, that wantons in the Field,
And fills the Neighb'ring Woods with horrid Fear,
When by the Hunter's Arts, at last beguil'd,
Strives with impetuous Rage, to break his Snare,
Fiercely, a while, his nervous Limbs resist,
Th'incircling Cords, regardless of his Pains,

                   Till

Till Nature's Strength, unable to persist,

Breathless, and Faint, falls drooping on the Plains.

Theocles.

Do's your Disorder, then from Love proceed?

Can that sweet Softness, such Affliction breed?

Strange !——

Is't possible the Nymph cou'd prove unkind?

Were all her Beauties to her Face confin'd?

Angel in Body, but all Fiend in Mind.

Some vain elated thing! ——

Phylander.

Rash THEOCLES!——

Your forward Zeal has wrong'd such Innocence,

Oh! Cælia, what will expiate this Offence!

Never when Wolves, attaqu'd my peaceful Plains,

Did Indignation fire my glowing Veins

With such impetuous Rage!——

My throbbing Breast can't bear the Calumny,

'Gainst Cælia speak, (by Heav'n!) 'tis Blasphemy;

It stabs my Soul, the Killing Words to bear;

My self! the World! I cou'd in pieces tear!

Theocles.

Theocles.

Such wild Confusion does thy Breast emove.
As does proclaim, indeed, you are in Love:
But yet——
If wrong I've offer'd, 'twas without design,
Tell me then now, wherein consists my Crime?

Phylander.

Will my Misfortunes never have an End!
I'ad lost my Peace, and now abus'd my Friend.
So Lunaticks, when Reason does dispense,
In Intervals, some little Rays of Sense,
Sadly bewail the various Ills they've done,
And both their Follies and Distemper moan.

But you, Great Youth, will easie Pardon deign,
You know the Malady does o'er me reign;
You know 'twas Zeal, pure Zeal for Cælia's Fame
Made me infringe our dear Platonick Flame.

Theocles

Theocles.

If Friendſhip fled, the Lover ſtill did ſtay;
And he I'm ſure, can very well diſplay,
What 'tis ſo much afflicts thy gen'rous Breaſt;
Murders thy Peace, and robs thee of thy Reſt;
Of him I'll aſk, if Cælia wa'n't unkind,
It muſt be that which grieves PHYLANDER's *Mind.*

Phylander.

Oh! 'tis in vain you ſtrive to anticipate,
What only He that feels can well relate.
Cælia unkind! No! ——
I have been bleſs'd, if Lovers bleſs'd can be,
With all that they eſteem Felicity:
Cælia, I've oft encircl'd in my Arms,
And by that Act. poſſeſs'd a Heav'n of Charms,
Found her the ſweeteſt, moſt engaging Maid,
Adorn'd with all her Sex e'er lovely made.
I cou'd have dwelt for ever in her Arms,
I cou'd have revell'd ever on her Charms.
Look, Look, THEOCLES! *to yon ſhady Grove,*
The ſilent Witneſs of our mutual Love:

Then

There did I oft dilate upon my Flame,

Whilst she with Blushes call'd me lovely Swain ;

Just like the little Lark, which mounts the Skies,

Filling the Air with its soft Melodies ;

Or the more pensive Musick of some Stream,

Where winding Strands, with'ts Currents intervene,

So did her Voice, in winning Accents move,

Whisp'ring repeated Vows of constant Love.

Oft when my bleating Flocks call'd me away,

Her blushing Cheeks she'd in my Bosom lay,

And trembling Coy, will you no longer stay :

Then with her tuneful Notes wou'd charm my Ears,

And use a thousand Arts to sooth my Cares.

Tell me then now, can she be call'd unkind,

Did ever Lover more Elizium find ?

Theocles.

What can the meaning of this Language be ?

Where is that Joy, that raving Exstasie!

Strange Paradox! Where is that Heav'n of Bliss,

Which Lovers boast they find in ev'ry Kiss ?.

Your doleful Plaints do shew the dire reverse,

The Cause of this I want you to rehearse. Phylander

Phylander.

Oh! THEOCLES ———

A Lovers Bliss, is all an idle Dream;
Thought on by none, that know what Love do's mean.
So fleeting, so precarious is his Joy,
Whilst Bliss he seeks, his Peace he do's Destroy.
His Life's one constant Scene of anxious Fears,
And e'ry Hour, adds, to his pungent Cares;
Each foolish Fancy, wracks his very Soul,
Ruffles his Breast, and Reason do's befool ;
He's ever Restless, ever is Opprest,
The Wise Man's Pity, and ev'ry Coxcombs Jest :
Meagre's his Visage, and his Mind deprest,
Depriv'd of Peace by Day, at Night of Rest,
A Lovers Wo's, can never be exprest.

Thrice Happy he, whose Noble Soul disdains,
To be a Captive made, to Cupid's Chains.
Thrice Happy he, that Spurns the mean desire,
And can be Happy in himself entire.

Theocles,

Theocles.

Are these the Raptures, idle Lovers boaſt!
Can Happineſs be found, where Peace is loſt!
Was Woman for a Plague then to us giv'n!
Is what we count a Hell! the Lovers Heav'n!
How ſad a Prey, is Youth, to flatt'ring Senſe,
Never convinc'd, but by Experience;
His blooming Health, his Blood with Vigor fills,
And lays him Open, to a Thouſand Ills:
Till fluſh'd by Natures Strength, ſome dire Exceſs,
Deprives him both of Life and Happineſs.

So the Young Heifer, to the Altar Bound
Is with the Pageantry, of Triumph Crown'd,
Till the ſharp Knife, its Vitals do's ſurprize,
And in deluſive Pomp, it Faints and Dies.

Oh ye Bleſt Pow'rs! whoſe Happy Manſions are
Out of the reach of Folly, and of Care,
Grant this Poor Swain, his Reaſon may recover,
And ne're Relapſe, into that Fool a Lover.

Panaretus

Panaretus having thus unloaded his Mind, and gratify'd *Dorinda*ѕ Requeſt determin'd to convey his Performance into her Hands by *Phylaſtratus* : And the better to Proſecute this Reſoluti-on, the firſt time he ſaw him, prepar'd the following Letter to Accompany it, *viz.*

Madam,

IT *is a common Obſervation, that Li-ſteners never hear good of them-ſelves. For my part, I ſhall very little regard the Force of the Proverb, (how-ever applicable it may be to me ;) If my Clandeſtine Intruſion upon the retired Dictates of theſe Youths, will afford you any Satisfaction. I muſt confeſs, 'tis a ſort of a diſmal Story, which* Phylander *gives, of the Paſſion you deſire me to De-ſcribe : But it ſeem'd to me ſo very ap-poſite to your Requeſt, that I cou'd not but recite it. I have had too large an Experience of your Ingenuity, in the leaſt to doubt of your Candor ; and therefore, tho' my Imperfections in the Recital be*
never

never fo apparent, I don't fear (if not an Excufe) at leaft a Pardon. I am Madam, your humble Servant to Command,

Panaretus.

Soon after *Panaretus* had wrote this Letter, and Pack'd it up with his Poem, in order to fend them to *Dorinda*: *Phylaftratus* having been Abfent from him now a full Week, thought high time to pay him another Vifit, and inquire whether he'd done the Task *Dorinda* had allotted him. Accordingly, he goes to their ufual Place of Rendezvous, and fends for him. *Panaretus* quickly obey'd his Summons, and knowing who 'twas that fent for him, came immediately, and brought his little Packet along with him. Being come, *Phylaftratus* foon gave him to underftand, that he was fhortly to go to *Dorinda*, and therefore firft came to him, to know whether he had made any Progrefs, in what She defired of him. *Panaretus* reply'd, "Yes he had done

done it, and made a moſt terrible Story
and by way of Precaution, ſaid, "If
"*Dorinda* ſhou'd ask whether I have ever
" a Miſtreſs nam'd *Cælia,* I wou'd not
"have you Inform her, becauſe I wou'd
"not have her have the leaſt Appre-
"henſion, that Name is any ways void
" of Fiction any more than the Reſt.
Phylaſtratus ſmiling at this, by an elu-
ſive Nod, ſeem'd to comply with his
Deſire, and after (having upon his leave
read the Paſtoral) put up the whole
Packet into his Pocket, promiſing it
ſhou'd not be long out of *Dorinda's*
Hands :   And having ſounded him a-
bout *Cælia,* to know whether he ſtill
retain'd the ſame Mind of her Innocence,
and upon his ſo doing, found no alteration in his Sentiments concerning
her, from what he expreſs'd when he
was with him, before he parted with
him, reſolving immediately to go to
Dorinda, and ſee what face things bore
with her ; and agreeably Poſted thither
with great Precipitation.

The nimbleneſs of his Steps, having
ſoon

foon brought him to her Door, after
an obfequious Wrap, he at once found
himfelf receiv'd, and conducted with
abundance of Joy by Old *Vulpone,* into
the Room were *Dorinda* was all alone.
Being feated, her Eagernefs to know,
whether *Panaretus* had comply'd with
her Requeft, gave no room for any thing
elfe; and therefore, She prefently. Ac-
cofted him with abundance of Queftions about *Panaretus's* Reception of her
Letter : "What he faid to it? Whe-
"ther he comply'd with it? Whether
"he'd done what She defir'd in it? With
a great many more of the fame Tendency.

Phylaftratus foon gave a Refolution to all her Queries, by pulling the
Packet out of his Pocket, and prefenting it to her, upon which, immediately opening the Letter, and Reading it,
and being willing to hear her Darling
Panaretus's Performance, with the greateft advantage; She defir'd *Phylaftratus*
to Read the Paftoral to her himfelf.
To this he agreed, with abundance of
Alacrity,

Alacrity, telling her " She cou'd not
" have Requeſted any thing of him,
" that he ſhou'd do with a greater De-
" light: Adding, he cou'd peruſe it
" for a whole Month together, with-
" out Satiety ; and proceeding to his
Task, Read it with that Inimitable
Beauty of Accent, and Turn of Oratory, as contributed no ſmall Matter
to Rivet the Soul of *Dorinda* if poſſible, yet faſter to her Beloved *Panare-*
tus. He omitted nothing, that the moſt
Ingenious Remarks upon it cou'd give,
to add ſome freſh Beauties to it.

There was not a Line, paſs'd without its Comment ; " And ſhou'd I tell
" you Madam, added he, the Circum-
" ſtances *Panaretus* was under when
" he Wrote this, it wou'd fill you yet,
" with greater Aſtoniſhment. *Dorinda*
having heard with an exceſs of Delight, the Numbers of her Beloved
Panaretus, ſet off with all the ſevera
Beauties of Wit, Oratory, and the
moſt ingaging Harmony of Accent
found her ſelf wholly Confirm'd in he
                                                preceeding

preceeding Thoughts, of *Panaretus's*
being under previous Engagements to
some other Lady ; and thinking *Phylastratus's* last Expreſſions, had given
her a favourable Opportunity, of knowing all particulars; Diſſembling the
concern She was under, as well as
She could, with an extorted Air of
Chearfulneſs, made *Phylaſtratus* a Reply as follows,——"The peculiar In-
"genuity of *Panaretus's* Performance,
"creates naturally a deſire in me, of
"knowing what theſe Circumſtances
"are, which renders it ſo much the
"more Surprizing. You to be ſure
can inform me. "Yes Madam, an-
"ſwer'd *Phylaſtratus*, I can ; and tho'
"I know I ſhall Infringe his deſire
"by doing it, yet I can't be Juſt to
"his Merits in omitting it. Whereupon he gave her a Summary account
of *Panaretus's* Amour with *Calia*, and
the Diſcoveries he himſelf had made
of her Falſhood to him. The various
emotions of Love, Joy, Diſdain and Indignation, that Revell'd in *Dorinda's*

F   Breaſt,

Breaft, whilft *Phylaftratus* told her this Story, render'd her quite Speechlefs, She did not know how to contain her felf under the hearing of it. The unfhaking conftancy of *Panaretus*, carry'd a thoufand Endearments along with it: The difcovery of her Rival afforded her infinite Satisfaction; but when fhe confider'd her, as fuch, and Falfe too, to *Panaretus*, her Blood boil'd with Difdain and Indignation. That fuch a Light, Contemptible, Falfe Girl, fhou'd Reign Afcendant in *Panaretus*'s Affections, and make her be Rejected, cut her to the very Soul. So Impetuous was the Rage fhe conceiv'd at it, and fo violent the Effect it had upon all her Paffions, that She cou'd not hide her Refentments even from *Phylaftratus*. *Calia*'s Falfhood and Ingratitude, was the fole Subject of her Difcourfe, for an Hour afterwards; She did not know when to defift Exclaiming againft her. *Phylaftratus* for his Part omitted no endeavours to keep up the Fuel, and having continu'd

tinu'd to Exagerate her Fury for a confiderable time, and finding Time now
call'd for his going away: He ask'd
her " Whether fhe wou'd be pleas'd to
" fend any thing by him, to *Panaretus*,
" it being now high time for him to
" think of going; defiring further, that
" if ever She faw *Panaretus*, not to tell
" him any thing he had told her, be-
" caufe he fear'd he wou'd be Angry,
" having defir'd him not to fpeak any
" thing of his Amour with her. *Dorinda*
promis'd to be Faithfully obfervant of
his laft Requeft, and as to his Firft, told
him, " She wou'd Beg him to ftay a
" little longer, becaufe fhe wou'd will-
" ingly fend Two or Three Lines by
" him, to *Panaretus*, to thank him for
" his Kindnefs. To which he very readily
Affenting, She retir'd and Wrote to
Panaretus as follows,

Generous *Panaretus*,

*I want Words to exprefs the many Ob
ligations I lye under to you. The Account you have given of the Ingenious*
Conference

Conference, you heard between the Witty, tho' unhappy Youth Phylander, and his Friend is in every part so ingagingly entertaining, that I shall never be able to make sufficient acknowledgments for it. The Language is so particularly moving, and the Name of Cælia, is mention'd with such an Ardent Emphasis, that ones Heart must be as hard as the Adamant inclos'd, not to be impress'd by it. Tell, Oh! Pray tell, that Lovely Shepherd Phylander, if ever you see him again, I sincerely Condole the Unhappiness he Labours under: And desire him, desire him from me, to Wear this Ring as a proper Emblem, of those Tempers he has to deal with. Yours, the Disconsolate,

Dorinda.

This Day Fortnight my Unkle goes out of Town, and stays Three Weeks, I shou'd be extremely oblig'd to you, if you wou'd take the Opportunity, of coming to see me during that Time.

Having wrote this, She pull'd a very fine Brilliant Ring from off her Finger, and Inclos'd it in it: And then

hasten'd

haften'd to *Phylaſtratus*, deſiring him to Excuſe her leaving him ſo long a-lone, and to Oblige her ſo far, as to give the Letter to *Panaretus*.

Phylaſtratus, promis'd punctually to perform her deſire, and having again Intreated her, never to tell *Panaretus* of what paſs'd between them; took his leave of her.

After he was gone, *Dorinda* retir'd, the better to ruminate on the many unuſual Circumſtances of *Panaretus*'s Amour. Tho' She cou'd not think, without the utmoſt Deteſtation, on *Calia*'s monſtrous Ingratitude: Yet She cou'd not but take a ſecret Delight to find She was ſo, ſince She was her Competitor in *Panaretus*'s Affection. Her wretched Falſhood She thought, wou'd render it much leſs difficult, to thruſt her out of his Heart; and therefore She concluded, if She cou'd but once make him ſenſible of it, her Work was Conſummate. The Methods of effecting this, were what She next revolv'd upon: And when

F 3 She

She reflected upon the strict Silence,
Phylastratus had injoyn'd her, it afforded her a little Perplexity. She found
her self so sensibly affected at *Celia's*
proceedings, that to be debarr'd Expressing her abhorrence against them,
was no small restraint upon her. Be-
sides, She imagin'd it wou'd mightily
endear her to *Panaretus*, cou'd She be
so Happy, as to give him Intelligence
of the Deception he was under; and
any thing, which her teeming Fancy,
cou'd Form to be pleasing to him,
necessarily carry'd several strong In-
ducements along with it. But her
strict Promise of Silence to *Phylastra-*
tus, was not to be Eluded, and tho'
She cou'd not have the Satisfaction of
giving her self, an eager Remonstrance
against *Celia's* Black Ingratitude : Yet
it afforded her some Consolation, when
She consider'd, that, that Friendship
which had led *Phylastratus* to discover
her so far, wou'd naturally excite him,
to Detect her even to *Panaretus* himself ; and therefore she resolv'd, at least
for

for fome time to let things take their
natural Courfe : Nurfing up in her
felf the pleafant hopes, of having fome
more advantagious Circumftances offer
themfelves unto her in a little time, and
thereby at once Sooth'd her vehement
Refentments againft *Cælia,* and in fome
meafure difipated her more Perplexing
Solicitude about *Panaretus.*

In the interim, *Phylaftratus* having
in his Accuftom'd manner, examin'd
the Contents of her Letter, inftantly
haften'd with it to *Panaretus* and gave
it to him : Parting from him as foon
as ever he had deliver'd it. For being fenfibly touch'd with the bafenefs
of *Cælia,* and mightily pleas'd to find
his Defign go on fo Succefsfully with
Dorinda, he refolv'd to lofe no time
nor opportunity, of making his Friend
fully fenfible of the Falfhood contain'd
in the former, and the Happinefs he
might poffefs, in the enjoyment of the
Latter. To this end therefore, he immediately went to *Sycophanta*'s Houfe,
enquiring with a feeming Air of Solici-

tude

tude after *Cælia,* omitting no Geſtures, that he thought their Vanity wou'd take for Indications, of his having an extraordinary deſire to ſee her. *Sy-cophanta* ſoon taking theſe Hints, im-mediately gave *Cælia* notice of his be-ing at her Houſe; and She having ad-juſted her Baubles, as well as poſſibly She cou'd, upon ſo ſhort warning, pre-ſented her ſelf to him, with all the al-luring Airs, that her ſhort Practice upon her Glaſs, and the natural Levi-ty of her Nature, cou'd any ways fur-niſh her with.

Phylaſtratus ſeeing her come ſailing towards him, as 'twere with a brisk Gale, immediately roſe up in order to carry on the Encounter with the better Advantage: And having ſaluted her, and elaborately Harangu'd her, upon her ſundry and various, and manifold, Beauties and Perfections, and thereby quitted the Room of *Sycophanta,* and her Emiſaries: He began artfully to expreſs a ſort of Diſfidence, that *Pana-retus* wou'd have the Preference in her Eſteem,

Efteem, notwithftanding his utmoft
Efforts to the contrary. Upon this,
Calia thinking there was nothing now
to be done, in order fully to fecure him;
but to give fome vehement Verbal Affurances, of his having no occafion to
have any doubts of that kind, immediately begain to be as full of her Vows
and Proteftations, as ever She was to
Panaretus. But he pretended to be ftill
under I know not what, Fears and
Doubts: She told him, She'd give him
any fatisfaction he wou'd require; upon which, he defir'd her to Carefs him
before *Panaretus*'s Face, and treat *Panaretus* with all the Marks of Scorn and
Difdain at the fame time. *Calia* very
willingly confented to this, promifing
to do it whenever he wou'd have her;
whereupon, feeming to be entirely
fatisfy'd, having thus fully gain'd his
purpofe, after a fhort Dalliance with
her, took his leave and parted with
her.

Whilft *Phylaftratus* was thus fully
employ'd, in detecting *Calia*'s Fallhood,

in

in such a manner as to leave her wholly
without Excuse: *Panaretus* was engag'd with an equal Diligence in the
Examination of *Dorinda*'s Letter. The
Witty Correspondency the Stile of it
bore to his own, and the noble Generosity She from thence took an opportunity to Exert; were things he cou'd
not pass by without various Reflections. And adding to these the incessant
Fatigue he had undergone, to get a
sight of *Cælia,* in order to know what
Sense She had of their so long Absence,
and the continual Disappointments
he found in his Attempts, with all the
Contempt and Ignominy that was, as
'twere showr'd upon him by *Sycophanta* and *Demogoga*: Revolving withal
upon some little Circumstances that
he observ'd even in *Cælia* herself, upon
his accidentally seeing her at some di-
stance in the Street, he began to entertain some light Thoughts of her being Unfaithful to him; and thereupon, Dilating a little further, upon the
many perplex'd Circumstances of his
Affairs,

Affairs, brought himself with little difficulty to believe, that her so long Abfenting her felf from him, was not altogether againft her own Will. No fooner had this Thought gain'd admittance into his Breaft, but that natural Jealoufy, which is always the neceffary Concomitant of a violent Affection ; made large Improvements of it, prefenting his Imagination with a Thoufand, either Real or imaginary Reafons, to confirm him in the Belief of its Truth, and letting flip nothing that cou'd contribute to Afflict and Torment his Mind. Now all that cou'd Fire his Refentments, Revell'd in his Breaft, Love, Jealoufy, Rage, Anger, Difpair, and all the other Impetuous Paffions of humane Nature, made their feveral Attacks upon his Soul ; here 'twas his Miferies feem'd to accumulate themfelves upon him, and he under a fatal Neceffity of finking under their Load. In this exceffive inquietude of Mind, he feem'd refolv'd wholly to abandon himfelf to his Grief.

Whe 1

When *Phylaſtratus* (having manag'd his Project with a pleaſing Succeſs, with both *Dorinda* and *Cælia,* and being willing *Panaretus* ſhou'd now reap the Fruits of his Labour;) was come to the Tavern where *Panaretus* and he uſually reſorted, and had order'd the Drawer to acquaint him, that he was there and wanted to ſpeak with him.

The Drawer having deliver'd his Meſſage, *Panaretus* promis'd to be with him preſently, and accordingly made his Appearance. When he was ſet down, *Phylaſtratus* obſerving an extraordinary diſorder in his Countenance, ask'd him, " How he did ? Upon which, Anſwering with an Air of ſecret Diſcontent : He proceeded to preſs him, to give a particular Account of the Concern he was under. Repoſing a particular Confidence in the Friendſhip of *Phylaſtratus,* he proceeded very frankly to Aſſign him the Cauſe of his preſent Trouble : Recounting all his proceedings of late with *Cælia,* with the Treatment he had

had receiv'd, and his particular Obſer-
vations upon *Cælia*'s Carriage; ſhowing throughout his whole Narative, all
the Indications of an enrag'd Jealouſy.
Phylaſtratus heard him tell his Story,
with the greateſt Pleaſure; and finding the Iron to be now hot, was reſolv'd to Strike, and thereupon eagerly Embracing him, he told him " His
" Fears were not groundleſs: *Cælia*
" was really Falſe, Inconſtant as Wind,
" the vileſt Crocadile not Hypocrite
" enough to be her Emblem. Par-
" don me, *Panaretus*, added he, if the
" Friendſhip I bore to you, natural-
" ly led me to make this Diſcovery;
and then he proceeded to tell him all
the particulars had paſs'd between him
and *Cælia*: Further alledging, that
he deſign'd Correſpondent to his laſt
Agreement with her, to let his own
Eyes be the Witneſs of her Falſhood,
with the Addition of the moſt ſtupid
Impudence. *Panaretus* ſtood like one
Thunder ſtruck at theſe Words; he
found the Arguments *Phylaſtratus* gave
carry

carry immediate Demonſtration along
with them, and tho' he cou'd not but
applaud his Friendſhip, yet he cou'd
not forbear with ſome Paſſion, to call
him a very unlucky Meſſenger; it was
a great while, before he cou'd ſtill his
Tumultuous Reſentments: But being
Reaſon'd into a kind of extorted calm-
neſs of Temper, by *Phylaſtratus*'s diligent Zeal for his Welfare; reſolv'd
(after he had vented himſelf with ſome
Paſſionate invectives againſt her Ingratitude.) to be himſelf a Spectator,
in the ſame manner as was agreed by
Phylaſtratus. After this, having fixt
the Time, it was further agreed, that
Phylaſtratus ſhou'd go firſt, and get
Cælia to come to him; ſoon after which
Panaretus was to follow; and then he
was to put her to the Teſt.

Matters being thus agreed, next
Morning *Phylaſtratus* goes in his wonted
manner to *Sycophanta*'s Houſe, and
ſends for *Cælia*; who quickly obeying
the Summons, and being Seated down
by him, and left alone by *Sycophanta*,
the

the better to carry on their Story:
After some little Dalliances had pass'd,
he began to Remind her of her Promise, when he was last with her;
telling her "He cou'd never be fully
"satisfy'd she had a real Esteem for
"him, till She had perform'd it. *Celia* altogether unapprehensive of any design in *Phylastratus*, told him " She
"wanted nothing but an Opportuni-
"ty of giving him the Satisfaction he
"requir'd; whereupon, seeming mightily pleas'd: Having talk'd away Half
an Hour, he found his Ears saluted
with the agreeable sound of a wrap
by *Panaretus* at the Door. No sooner
was he enter'd, but *Sycophanta* having
spied him, came running almost Breathless, telling them with great Confusion, *Panaretus* was come, asking them
both how She shou'd shove him off.
Celia willing to show an extraordinary readiness, to oblige her new Gallant,
bid her let him come in: And *Phylastratus* seeming with some Reluctancy to comply with the Motion; he
was

was accordingly, with a pouting Look,
conducted in by *Sycophanta*. *Panaretus*
being enter'd the Room, where his
Friend and *Cælia* were, diffembling his
inward Difcontent, as well as poffibly
he cou'd, immediately addreffing himfelf to *Cælia*, told her, "She was grown
"a great Stranger. At which, fcorn-
fully anfwering him, "So much the
"better. He ask'd her, "What he
"had done to merit fuch Treatment?
"I am not oblig'd (anfwer'd fhe) to
"to give my Reafons to fuch fcribbling
"Fellows as you. If my Company is
"troublefome to you, (reply'd *Panare-*
"*tus*) you may foon be rid on't. The
"fooner the better, anfwer'd fhe. Upon which, *Panaretus* going to quit the
Room, *Phylaftratus* privately tip'd him
the Wink to ftay a little longer; and
thereupon taking *Cælia* by the Hand,
faid, "I doubt you're angry, Madam.
"I don't love to fee you difpleas'd; I
"fhould be very forry if I thought I
"was burdenfome to you. Pray, Sir,
anfwer'd *Cælia*, with an exceffive wanton

ton Air, "don't harbour such a Thought.
Upon which, *Panaretus*, unable to be
any longer a Spectator, leaving them,
she turn'd her self to *Phylastratus*, smi-
ling upon him, and telling him, "Now
" she hop'd she had given full satisfa-
" ction. Yes, answer'd *Phylastratus*,
(springing from her in a Rage, and
following his Friend) " and him too, I
" hope.

This sudden Alteration very much
surpriz'd her; but being of a Nature
too savage to entertain any thing like
Remorse, tho' she cou'd not think of
losing both her Sparks, without the
most stinging Regret, yet such a sort
of stupid Imperiousness of Nature
reign'd predominant over her, as render'd her obstinately resolv'd, not so
much as to seem concern'd. She was
not insensible now, that all *Phylastratus*'s Proceedings were purely to try
her all along; but the same Malignancy of Nature, which had precipi-
tated her to make such a large Disco-
very of her self, erac d all the common
Sen-

Sentiments of Shame wholly out of her Mind, and at once hurry'd her, desperately to persist, both in her Guilt and Folly. And here we'll leave her, the better to trace the Proceedings of her two Sparks.

Pylaftratus having left *Cælia,* made all imaginable haste to get to *Panaretus,* and having overtaken him, told him, " They would drink one Glass before " they parted. *Panaretus*'s Mind being under infinite Disorder at *Cælia*'s Proceedings, ·wou'd willingly have declin'd drinking with him at that time, but *Phylaftratus*'s Importunity admitting of no Denial, they went both together to a Tavern.

When they were seated, *Phylaftratus* observing an exceeding Pensiveness hung over *Panaretus*'s Countenance, he earnestly entreated him to shake off all irksome Thoughts about a Girl that so little deserv'd his Concern; largely inculcating the Happiness it was to him, to perceive this before 'twas too late; pressing him further, then to vent all his

trouble

trouble about her in a Letter; telling him, becaufe it fhou'd be Satyr enough, he'd help him dictate it; urging, that his writing to her then, wou'd give Eafe to his Mind, and, he hop'd, prevent his breaking another Night's Reft about her. To which *Panaretus*, after abundance of Perfuafion, comply'd. *Phylaftratus* immediately calling for a Pen Ink and Paper, looking over *Panaretus* whilft he wrote, the better to promp this Refentments, caus'd him to vent the tumultuous Paffion from his Breaft in the following Lines, *viz.*

Vain Ungrateful Girl,

I *Shou'd have as little Senfe, as you have common Modefty, if I fhou'd think this Paper, wou'd either rouze your Confcience, or make you blufh: No,* Cælia! *I know now, (tho' once I cou'd not have believ'd it) that you have neither Confcience nor Shame.* Vain Thing! *Thy Folly will prove as great as thy Falfhood. For my part, I banifh thee henceforth, ever*
from

from my Heart : Thou shalt be as Contemp-
tible as thou hast been Perfidious to my
Soul; and because I'll be nobly reveng'd
on you, I'll forgive you: So, farewel, Foo-
lish Girl, may thy Crime be thy only Pu-
nishment, and Heaven forgive thee as I
do. Your vain Imagination, I know, has
form'd to your self one you like better, but
you will never have a more Faithful,
Truer Lover, than always has been,

PANARETUS.

PANARETUS having by writing
this, a little relax'd his Mind, from
that load of Anxiety that before so
entirely possess'd it, soon began, by the
brisknes of his Aspect, to give his
Friend some Hopes that the Thoughts
of Cælia wou'd in a little time quite
work off All his Faculties began to
make very great Advances to their
wonted Vivacity, and that acoute Vexation, which had, as 'twere, overspread
all the Powers of his Soul, seem'd now
to give place to the more pleasing Sentiments

iments of a generous Gratitude. He vas not infenfible, that this happy Re-olution of his Paffions, was purely wing to the friendly Vigilance of *Phy-iftratus*, and therefore he thought he ou'd never make fufficient Acknow--dgments to him for it. " Oh *Phy-laftratus!* cry'd he, (with all the en-dearing Expreffions of Love and Friendfhip) how can I be grateful enough, for the Pains you have taken? Oh! Shocking Thought! Why? Oh! Why muft I feem to be falfe to one, who has been fo kind, fo true to me? le went on with thefe paffionate Ex-lamations, for a confiderable Time : eing touch'd with the moft perplexing ear, that if ever *Phylaftratus* fhou'd ifcover his Proceedings with *Dorinda*, e wou'd impute not only Falfhood, ut the higheft Ingratitude to him.

Phylaftratus clearly feeing thro' the mbiguity of thefe Expreffions, and ful-'apprehending the Caufe of his Trou-le, was unable longer to let him con-nue his Doubts, and therefore earneft-ly

ly embracing him, cry'd out, " Ceaſe,
" O ceaſe! my dear *Panaretus*, to per-
" plex thy Noble Breaſt, any more in
" this kind; ſooner ſhall the Ocean
" ſtop its Courſe, the Sun ſtand ſtill,
" and all Nature be revers'd, than I
" entertain the leaſt diffident Thought
" of thy Faithfulneſs.   I am not inſen-
" ſible of thy Generous Conſtancy, both
" to me, and the Ungrateful *Cælia*.'Twas
" the knowledge of this made me put
" that falſe Girl to the Teſt. I cou'd not
" think a Light Inconſtant worthy of
" *Panaretus*, and therefore I reſolv'd to
" try her, as you find.   'Tis I, my dear
" *Panaretus*, that am the only Agreſ
" ſor.   And hereupon he proceeded to
give him an Account of his opening al
the Letters that had paſs'd between
him and *Dorinda*; recounting every Circumſtance from Firſt to Laſt; adding
further, That he had purpoſely taken
ſo much Pains to diſcover *Cælia*, the
better to render him able, at once to
make both himſelf and *Dorinda* happy.

Panaretu

Panaretus being under the greateſt ſurprize imaginable, at what *Phylaſtra-us* related to him, found it no little difficulty for him to perſuade himſelf into the reality of what he heard. But *Phylaſtratus* having told him the Sub-ects of ſeveral of the Letters which had aſs'd between him and *Dorinda,* and hown him the Seal he had got grav'd, n order to counterfeit his, and thereby eft him no room to doubt, ſmiling at he Oddneſs of the Story, he ask'd him, ' Whether *Dorinda* was any ways privy ' to his Proceedings? *Phylaſtratus* an-wer'd him, No, and deſir'd him fur-her, not to acquaint her with the Diſ-overy he had all along made, becauſe e was apprehenſive it would extremely erplex her, and, beſides, render him ncapable of carrying on the Plot any urther. *Panaretus* promis'd to do as e'd have him ; telling him, " He free-' ly reſign'd her up to him, wiſhing he ' might have more Happineſs in her, ' than he had had in *Cælia.* *Phylaſtra-us* reply'd, " He had long ago found
" no

" no other Notion of Happiness, in re-
" ference to *Dorinda*, than by being In-
" strumental to conduct her into the
" Arms of her belov'd *Panaretus*; and
" therefore desir'd him to think of no-
" thing, but compensating his loss of
" *Cælia*, by the full Enjoyment of the
" much more deserving and lovely *Do-*
" *rinda.*

This generous Declaration of *Phyla-*
stratus, was acknowledg'd with all the
endearing Expressions of the most enlarg'd Gratitude, by *Panaretus*; he
thought he cou'd never sufficiently express his Thankfulness, nor expatiate
enough on the Heroickness of his whole
Procedure. That sordid Narrowness o
Soul, which is asham'd to own a Benefit, when really conferr'd, never yet infected him. As he had a Soul large e-
nough to be beneficent himself, so he
cou'd never be found so meanly Invidious, as to detract from any thing that
was truly great in another. But *Phyla-*
stratus desiring him to desist any further Enlargements of this kind, telling
him

him, "If any thing he had done, me-
"rited his Panegyrick, he had copy'd
"it from him, and therefore he hop'd
"he'd excuse those troublesome Inter-
"ruptions among Friends, Compliments,
"and fully satisfie himself, he esteem'd
"himself amply rewarded for whatever
"he'd done, if thereby he prov'd ser-
"viceable to him.)

Panaretus, with some Reluctancy, was
content to be silent. And thereupon
taking his Glass, joyn'd with *Phylastratus* in drinking *Dorinda*'s Health, strictly promising the most inviolable Friendship towards him. *Phylastratus* return'd
his Promises in equivalent Terms, and
having, with infinite satisfaction, observ'd his Mind now to be all over calm
and serene, he merrily ask'd him for
the Letter he had wrote to *Cælia*, telling
him, "He'd either carry it himself to
"her, or send his Man with it, that
"they might be the better assur'd she
"receiv'd it. Whereupon *Panaretus* gave
it him unseal'd, desiring him to seal it
with his old ploting Seal. So after several
G   other

other such facetious Turns had pafs'd between them, they parted for that time.

Phylaftratus having hitherto carry'd
on his Plot, with a continu'd Series of
Succefs, and having got *Panaretus*'s
Letter to *Cælia* in his poffeffion; he refolv'd to go and make *Dorinda* a Partner
of that Pleafure he found dilate fo fenfibly in his own Breaft. He knew the
News of *Panaretus*'s having cafhier'd
Cælia, wou'd be exceedingly grateful to
her; and therefore he determin'd to lofe
no time before he had given her the a-
greeable Intelligence. No fooner therefore had he parted from *Panaretus*, but he
pofted directly to her Houfe, and being
conducted to the Room where fhe was,
prefently began his Narrative of what
had pafs'd between *Panaretus* and *Cælia*.

Dorinda receiv'd both him and his
News with the greateft fatisfaction;
and having with infinite Delight perus'd
Panaretus's Letter, ask'd him, "What
" he defign'd to do with it? Do with
" it! Madam, (anfwer'd he) why fend
" it to her by my Footman, whom
I've

" I've order'd to call on me, in' order to
" carry it to her. Will your Footman,
" then, come to you here? said *Dorinda.*
" Yes, Madam, anſwer'd he. Upon
which, *Dorinda* mightily pleas'd her ſelf
with the Mortification 'twou'd be to *Cælia*, to receive it from the hands of *Phylaſtratus*'s Footman; largely entertaining
both her ſelf and him with a thorough
Deſcant on every Circumſtance of it,
till they found themſelves interrupted by
Phylaſtratus's Man's knocking at the
Door. Being enter'd, and enquiring for
his Maſter, *Phylaſtratus* order'd him,
before *Dorinda*'s Face, to carry the Letter to *Cælia*, and deliver it into none
but her Hand ; to which promiſing to
be ſtrictly obſervant, he diſmiſs'd him.

When he was gone, *Phylaſtratus* a-
gain reſum'd the Diſcourſe with *Dorinda*, they were before engag'd in, and
having fully recounted to her *Panaretus*'s Behaviour throughout the whole
Interview, between him and *Cælia*,
ſounding thereby the ſecret Springs of
her Heart; and finding abundance of

repeated

repeated Confirmations, both by her Words and Gestures, that she was still entirely possess'd in favour of his Friend; pretending he took that Opportunity of calling on her as he came that way, because he thought the Revolution that had pass'd in *Panaretus*'s Affairs was so very extraordinary, that he cou'd not (having before given her a short Account of his Amour) but acquaint her with it; after usual Ceremonies pass'd, he parted with her.

After he was gone, *Dorinda* exceedingly delighted her self, in revolving on what he had related to her; she fully persuaded her self, that now all her Storms were totally blown over, and all her succeeding Hours were to be fann'd with the engaging Breezes of gentle *Zephyrs.* She began now, in a sort of pleasing Delirium, to anticipate the several abstracted Delights she thought wou'd necessarily accrue to her, in the entire Enjoyment of her belov'd *Panaretus*; no Circumstances that the most enlarg'd Fancy cou'd form, were pass'd by

by without some pleasing Reflections.
Like the exalted Joy of Mariners just
'scap'd the various Terrors of some im-
pending Rock, so did her languid Spirits again revive, and fresh Vigour fill'd
her chearful Veins. All her preceeding
Vexation and Disappointments, were
now pass'd over in Oblivion, as if they
were only the airy Phantoms of an irksome Dream that is past. Nothing entertain'd her Thoughts, but the pleasing
Prospect of a happy Futurity; and
so intensely was her Imagination fixt
on the several delightful Scenes in the
Prospect, that nothing else cou'd be
found of sufficient force, to justle them
out of her Mind.

Phylastratus, on the other side, with
all that sublimated Pleasure, which truly great and generous Souls enjoy in being Beneficent and Kind; reflected upon what he had done. So enlarg'd and
noble was the Emulation he had, of
showing as great Evidences of a real
and disinterested Friendship, as he had
found *Panaretus* so bright an Example

G 3   of,

of, that 'twas his continual ſtudy, how he might, if poſſible, do ſomething that wou'd outvie him. The Succeſs there-fore, he had hitherto had, and the pro-bability conſequent thereupon, of his being likely to be inſtrumental in a very large degree, to the Happineſs of his Friend, were things that afforded a chearing Banquet to his Mind. So far was he from that abject Narrowneſs of Spirit which determines all its Acts of Kindneſs within the little Circle of Self-Intereſt ; that he took a ſort of generous Pride, not only in being Friendly, but in hiding it when he had done. He thought the Benefactors being unknown, made the Benefit the greater; and was ſo far from the contemptible Loquacity of thoſe, who dun the Ears of all about them with a tedious Repetition of all the good Offices they've done ; that he as induſtriouſly conceal'd them, as if the immediate Conſequence of their being known, were Shame and Pu-niſhment. The inward Complacency and Satisfaction of his own Mind, were

were esteem'd, by him, an ample Reward; and therefore, (being encourag'd hitherto by a pleasing Success)
he resolv'd not to desist prosecuting his
Design, till he had at once consummated
both it, and the Happiness of his Friend
and *Dorinda.* His Mind, having regal'd
it self, with these, and the like entertaining Reflections, and laid down a
Scheme of his future Procedure, now
found it self diverted by some Intelligence that was given him 'of his Man's
being return'd, and having deliver'd
the Message he sent him about, and then
waited to know what was further his
Pleasure; upon which, sending Word
for him to come to him, and he thereupon presenting himself, he examin'd
him thoroughly about his management
of his Errand.

His Man told him, " According to
" his Command, he went to the Lady,
" and upon his Enquiry after her, was
" conducted to her, and having tho-
" roughly inform'd himself that she was
" the Person he sent him to, agreeable

" to

" to his Order he gave her the Letter;
" whereupon, continu'd he, she imme-
" diately open'd it, and read it over
" with abundance of Attention; upon
" which blushing, and looking excee-
" dingly confus'd, she ask'd me whether
" you sent me. I reply'd, Yes, where-
" upon she hastily rush'd from me, and
" shut the Door upon me, giving me
" no Answer at all.

Having heard the whole Account,
he dismiss'd him, afterwards mightily
pleasing himself with the Evidences *Cælia* had given of her secret and stinging
Vexation.

Whilst *Dorinda*, and *Phylastratus*,
were thus differently entertaining their
Thoughts, with the various Turns and
Vicissitudes of things; *Panaretas*'s Mind
was no less fully employ'd. *Dorinda's*
generous Affection, *Phylastratus's* unexampl'd Friendship, and *Cælia's* black
Falshood and Ingratitude, were in their
several Turns fully canvass'd in his
Mind. *Dorinda* appear'd strongly attractive of his Affection, and he cou'd
not

not but entertain some Thoughts of offering it, as the just Stipends of her extraordinary Merits; but the Part *Phylastratus* had acted, seem'd, at present, to lay abundant greater Obligations upon him. Here he was quite amaz'd in the Contemplation; there was something in its every Part, gave a vast Space for his most stretch'd Imagination to range upon; that he shou'd bear with patience *Dorinda*'s slighting his Suit; preferring him; making a Messenger; a Tool of him, with abundance more, that might be ennumerated of that kind; these he cou'd not but think were shocking Tryals; but that he shou'd know all this, and yet go on in such a Noble, such an Exalted Manner, to act the Tenderest, the most Endearing Offices of Friendship, even to his Rival, this he thought was strictly peculiar to him, and evidenc'd him something more than Humane. Actions, like these, he thought, so largely assimulated themselves to the Divine Nature, that it must necessarily be, the great Mover of them: But

G 5   when

when he yet trac'd him further, and
with the highest Astonishment, reflected on the Pains and Fatigue he'd been
at, to detect *Calia's* Falshood, and had
yet further still enhanc'd the unbounded
Nature of his Generosity, by resigning
up even *Dorinda*, it struck such an enlarg'd Sense of Gratitude on his Soul,
and fixt so many bright Ideas of him on
his Mind, as render'd it hard for him to
quit them, without making some slight
Excursions into Superstition ; so vast
was the Opinion he had conceiv'd of
him. As to *Calia*, he cou'd not, indeed,
easily forget her, but her late Proceedings had so fully errac'd all his wonted
Affection to her out of his Breast, that
he entertain'd no other Thoughts about
her, but what carry'd with them the
accutest Sense of Scorn and Contempt.
He was so far from being in any Pain
concerning her, that he look'd upon
even her very Falshood, to be the immediate Instrument of an Omniscient
Providence ; and after he had fully attended to the several Circumstances of
his

his Affairs, at that Juncture, and found
them all, as 'twere, with one Voice,
plead *Dorinda*'s Cause, was refolv'd to
fall in with the Overtures she made him,
and transfer that Affection *Celia* had
fo ungratefully abus'd, entirely upon
her.

A Fortnight's time now being full
paft, fince *Dorinda* fent her laft Letter
to *Panaretus*, *Phylaftratus* (knowing that
to be the Time, *Vulpone*, according to
her Account was to go into the Country) thought it now high Time to found
Panaretus's Refolution, whether he defign'd, agreeable to *Dorinda*'s Defire,
to give her a Vifit, during her Unkle's
Abfence ; and the better to inform himfelf, repair'd inftantly to him. After
he had fent for him in his ufual manner,
and they had reciprocally fatisfy'd each
other in the common Interrogatives of
Friends that have been fometime abfent
from each other : He went on to enquire, "What his Refolutions were with
"refpect to *Dorinda* ? *Panaretus* re-
"ply'd, he was really fo all over poffefs'd
                              "with

" with Aſtoniſhment, at the unprece-
" dented Generoſity of his Proceedings,
" that he was incapable of making any
" Anſwer.   Deſiſt, I beſeech you, ſaid
" *Phylaſtratus*, any further Compli-
" ments, and conſider, not ſo much
" what you are pleas'd to call my Gene-
" roſity, as the great Affection *Dorin-*
" *da* bears towards you ; conſider what
" ample Rewards ſhe'll return your moſt
" enlarg'd Affection, and never let the
" brighteſt Lady in the Univerſe be loſt,
" under the Pretence of paying a De-
" ference to me.   I wou'd not have you
" think I perſuade you thus, becauſe I
" have not a juſt Senſe of her great Per-
" fections : No ! I am not ſo ſtupid
" neither ; had I had the Happineſs of
" impreſſing her Heart, with any thing
" like that Paſſion ſhe ſuſtains for you,
" the greateſt Monarch on Earth ſhou'd
" not have tore her from me :   Even
" *Panaretus* himſelf, I wou'd not have
" brook'd a Rival ; but ſince All-wiſe
" Heaven ſeems to allot her as a Bleſſing
" peculiar to you ; I chearfully acqui-
                              " eſce,

" esce, and am so far from envying, that
" I heartily congratulate your Happi-
" ness : Live happy therefore with
" your lovely *Dorinda*, whilst I shall
" have this Felicity, however, to know
" 'tis my Friend, 'tis *Panaretus* enjoys
" her. *Panaretus* seem'd to turn this
engaging Oratory of *Phylastratus*, with
all the winning Rhetorick that Love,
Gratitude, and Friendship cou'd suggest,
promising him to go and visit *Dorinda*,
during her Unkle's Absence ; and to be
strictly observant of whatever else he
shou'd require : At which, *Phylastratus*
expressing Abundance of Satisfaction,
after he had made him give him several
strong Assurances of his going to see her
the next Day ; he parted with him,
infinitely pleas'd at the Success he had
found.

Agreeable to this Appointment, *Panaretus* (having inform'd himself that
Vulpone was gone out of Town) went
to pay *Dorinda* a Visit. Being arriv'd
at her House, and conducted to her
Appartment, by *Isabella*, he found her
in

in the utmoſt Confuſion at his Appear.
ance : Tho' to ſee him, was what ſhe
earneſtly coveted ; yet, ſo accute was
the Reflection of what had paſs'd between them, and ſo great the Aſcendancy he bore over every Power of her
Soul : That the natural Vivacity of her
Genius ſeem'd quite bore down, by his
Preſence. She knew not how to Face
a Gentleman, with whom ſhe had carry'd on, what ſhe cou'd not but eſteem,
a continu'd Series of Extravagancies;
tho' ſhe had hitherto always thought
her Pen encounter, a Matter of the
higheſt Difficulty to manage : Yet
now ſhe ſenſibly experienc'd how much
his perſonal Appearance ſurmounted it.
'Twas in vain for her to attempt, even
to feign ſome ſort of Reſolution, the
wonted Briskneſs of her Fancy, wholly
abandon'd her, and the Native Beauties
of her Modeſty, repell'd its utmoſt Sallies, and at once lock'd up her Tongue,
and over-ſpread her Face with profound
Silence, and confus'd Bluſhes.

Pani.

Panaretus having fully obferv'd her, eafily guefs'd the many Perturbations of her Breaft, by the feveral Changes of her Countenance ; and therefore ad-drefs'd himfelf to her, in all the moft tender and indulgent Expreffions he cou'd poffibly contrive, to footh the various Cares fhe feem'd fo fenfibly loaded withal. "Ceafe, I beg you, "Madam, faid he, all further Difor-"der, and let me not have this additi-"onal Misfortune to my other, to find "my Company diftafteful, even to "you. The Multitudes of Ills, that "have feem'd hitherto to have befet my "every Verge of Life ; have yet afford-"ed me this Satisfaction, that I, and I "alone, have been the Sufferer : But, "to find my felf at laft, the unhappy "Caufe of fo great Diforder, in a "Breaft fo noble, fo truely vertuous as "yours, adds frefh Pungency to my, "Afflictions, and renders them infup-"portable. Blufhes are the Symptoms "of bodeing Guilt : Why then is the "eternal Nature of Things inverted ?

"How

" How comes it, a Soul ſo unſtain'd, ſo
" imaculate, as yours preſents the amaz-
" ing Scene unto my Eyes ? *Dorinda,* having by the greatneſs of her Attention
to what he ſaid, a little ſuſpended the
many Paſſions that before attacqu'd her
found her ſelf now no longer able to
ſuſtain the Violence of their Onſets;
and therefore rallying her confus'd
Forces together, as well as poſſibly ſhe
cou'd, paſſionately rejoyn'd, as follows. " Oh! *Panaretus,* tho' thy win-
" ning Eloquence wou'd charm the very
" Angels; yet, vainly does it ſtrive to
" ſhade the dazling Rays of more ſub-
" ſtantial Reaſon; Bluſhes you truly
" ſay, are Signs of bodeing Guilt; Truths
" ſo flagrant are not to be eluded ; and
" tho' I can't but gratefully applaud the
" indulgent Pity of your Wit ; yet, I find
" it equally impoſſible to diſſemble the
" inward Sentiments of my own conſci-
" ous Breaſt; in vain do we endeavour
" for to fly, when angry Conſcience
" hunts us : Nature itſelf conſpires a-
" gainſt the harden'd Wretch, who
" thinks

" thinks to skreen his Crimes from Ven-
" geance, and spreads a dire Confusion
" o'er that Face, whose faultring
" Tongue wont own its vile Offences.
She wou'd have proceeded, but *Panaretus* quite impatient, to find the ge-
nuine Intent of his Expressions so wittily inverted ; eagerly embracing her
in his Arms, entreated her in the most
moving Language, to banish all such
irksome, groundless Thoughts from
her Mind, earnestly desiring her to believe, he had entertain'd no other
Thoughts of her Conduct, but what
were vastly wide of those Construc-
tions, she so industriously put upon
'em her self. Here 'twas he omitted
nothing that the quickest Fancy cou'd
furnish him with, to sooth the Concern
she was under ; Painted in the most
beautiful Forms, his inward Sentiments
of her Merits ; and gave so many evident Testimonies of the sincerity of
his Mind, as wholly dispers'd the many
perplexing Doubts she labour'd under,
and regal'd her Breast with the more
agree-

agreeable Emotious of Content, and Satisfaction.

Our Couple having carry'd on their Enterview thus far to their mutual Satisfaction; and fully, as well as happily communicated their Minds to each other (after they had spent an Hour or two in those pleasing Endearments, that naturally attend Meetings of this Kind) reciprocally agreed to concert some Measures for their future Procedure. The Prosecution of their Amour, they both concluded wou'd necessarily be retarded if not totally hinder'd, shou'd her Unkle *Vulpone* be acquainted with it; the mighty Hopes he had conceiv'd of *Phylastratus*'s large Fortune, they were sensible wou'd not be easily superceeded; and therefore they resolv'd industriously to hide it from him, and refer the Consumation of their Nuptials, 'till the Command of her Fortune came in her own Power. Upon this general View of their Affairs, easily collecting that they cou'd not so frequently enjoy each others Company, as they desir'd; they soon foon came to a Refolution of making the utmoft Improvements of their prefent Advantages they poffibly cou'd; and therefore, quickly agreed to take the prefent Opportunity of *Vulpone*'s Abfence, fully to eftablifh their whole Scheme and give themfelves fome particular Gratifications, which cou'd not well be manag'd when he came Home. A-mongft the many other Particulars that were the Confequence of this Determination; one was a fet Appointment, which they made, to Meet in fome private Walks: The Day fixt was the third Day following, after which Affignation, having given each other the moft earneft, and repeated Affurances of inviolable Affection, they parted for that Time.

Dorinda, immediately retir'd to entertain her Immagination more freely upon the feveral pleafing Amufe ments of what had pafs'd: Whilft *Panaretus,* no lefs Bigg with what had been tranfacted, directed his Steps with no little Precipitation, to the
usual

uſual Place of Rendezvous; and inſtantly ſent for his Friend *Phylaſtratus,*
in order to give him the pleaſing Narrative of his whole Proceedings. *Phylaſtratus* quickly obeying the Summons,
ſoon gave him an Opportunity of beginning his Story, and having, with a
delightful Attention, heard a full Account of every Part of their Converſe,
expreſs'd an infinite Satisfaction at the
whole, but eſpecially at the Appointment he had made of going abroad with
her. This ſaid he, is a Circumſtance
affords me an exceeding Delight, becauſe I have a Mind from hence to take
an Opportunity of putting her at once to a
ſhocking Tryal, and giving an intire So-
lution to all her Fears about me for the
future. And thereupon deſir'd *Panaretus*
ſo to order Matters, that he might meet
them out together, ſeemingly accidental, the particular Methods of affecting
which, in caſe he was willing, he told
him, they wou'd then conſult about.
Panaretus very readily complying with
the Propoſal, they mutually agreed, that
he

he fhou'd take her out to t'other fide the Water, and between Three and Four a clock in the Afternoon, crofs over again with her to *Whitehall*, in order to take a Walk with her in the *Park* ; where, in a feeming accidental manner, he wou'd meet them both in the *Mall* ; by which they fhou'd have the Pleafure of feeing the Surprize fhe wou'd be under, and afterwards of carrying on their Friendfhip in a more open, and to her, lefs perplexing manner. Having thus fully concerted their Meafures, they reciprocally recogniz'd the Friendfhip they had as yet fo inviolably continu'd, by a chearing Glafs, and after having given each other feveral repeated Affurances of their acting agreeable to their Appointment, took leave of each other.

Whilft *Panaretus* and *Phylaftratus* were thus laying their Stratagem, *Dorinda* was no lefs bufied in the Reflection upon what had pafs'd between her and the Former. The Thoughts of her Walks with him regal'd her Mind with

fo

so many pleasing Amusements, as render'd it very difficult for her to admit any thing else into it. Her fruitful Imagination dress'd it up in so many delightful Circumstances, that the Intervention of Three Days seem'd to her a very tedious Suspence; and not One Minute of it was pass'd over without a sort of anticipation of the Felicity she propos'd then to enjoy. She esteem'd her approaching Happiness so wholly consummate, as not in the least to be incident to the common Vicissitude of Things, and such an unaccustom'd Serenity possess'd her Breast, and sooth'd her wonted Diffidence, that she knew not now what it was so much as to fear a Disappointment. All other Business was so wholly swallow'd up in the Preparation for this, as if no other Part of Life were at all to be regarded; 'till Time (having heighthen'd her Expectations, by the nearer Approaches of the so long wish'd for Hour) call'd on her more immediately to fit her self for the Reception of her Gallant. And having

gain'd

gain'd Intelligence by her little fide
Utenfil, that *Panaretus* was nigh making his Appearance, prefently adjufted
all her Attire (with all the pleafing Expectation of an eager Bridegroom, when
rigging himfelf on his Nuptial Morn)
in Order to give him the more ready
Attendance when he came. The Morning being now come, and the Hour
appointed very near, *Panaretus* having
procur'd a Coach, order'd it to drive
immediately to *Dorinda*'s Door ; which
being prefently arriv'd at, he found her
with the greateft Alacrity in the World,
ready to fly into his Arms.

The mutual Defire they both had of
profecuting their Ambulatory Enter-
prize, made them very brief in their
Complements; and therefore, after
fome fhort Salutations had pafs'd,
he conducted her into the Coach,
ordering the Coach - Man to drive
them to *Salisbury* - Stairs. Having
receiv'd his Inftructions, and mount-
ed his Seat, our *Jehu* foon gave his Fare
fuch jumbling Treatment, as put *Pa-*

naretus

naretus under the pleasing Necessity of locking *Dorinda* fast in his Arms, the better to fence her from the surly Wraps of the Side of their noisy Receptacle, and give her a sort of Specimen of the consumate Bliss of Love. Mean while our *Castigator*, regardless of what was done within, and fearless of Danger from without, drove on 'till he came to the Place allotted; when having by a strenuous Tug, put Period to the Career of his reeking Drudges, with a clumsey Jump, and blund'ring Stagger, makes his Approaches to the Door, where pulling of off his Hat, and scratching of his Noddle, by the Help of an aukard Shrug, and ugly Grimace, gave them to understand they was arriv'd at *Salisbury*-Stairs. *Panaretus*, upon this Information, having help'd *Dorinda* out of the Coach, immediately deposited into the Fellow's Hands, Six-Pence more than his Fare; whereupon, with the wonted Insolence, and Ingratitude of his Fraternity, he saluted him with, " a G---d bless you Master give

" me

" me t'other Sice; upon which, being answer'd with a sound knock on the Pate he brush'd off with what he'd got. No sooner had he thus quitted himself of one Blockhead, but they found themselves assaulted with at least Twenty more; Yelping and Bellowing with a hedious Out-cry, as if they had a mind to break the Drum of their Ears: One Howling out like a foolish Puppy, or ill tun'd Bag-Pipe, "Scullers! Scullers! Whilst another (that you might have the very Quintisence of Discord) roar'd in your Ears, (with a Voice as deep as the Diapason of St. *Paul's*) "Oars! Oars! being quite stunn'd with the repetition of this Mob Dialect, before they cou'd be heard which they'd chosen, at last, *Panaretus* found an opportunity of being heard to say Oars: Whereupon an Old Grizzl'd Fellow, with every Stud of his Beard, as thick almost as a Crow's Quill, lugging him by the Arm, Cry'd Here! Here. And by the assistance of strong Lungs, and ill Language, made him intirely his Property. Having

H thus

thus got the Fare, and huddl'd them both into his Boat, he immediately follow'd, quitting the Shoar with Fire in his Looks, and Menaces on his Tongue. *Panaretus* having feated *Dorinda* now pretty regularly, and exceedingly diverted both himfelf and her, at the Scurrility of their Pilot: Was going to give him Orders where to carry them, but before he cou'd fully tell him, found himfelf and *Dorinda* accofted with the engaging Appellations of " Whore and Rogue, with abundance more " of the fame kind. *Panaretus* altogether unable to return their Water Rhetoric, was content to Laugh heartily at what he cou'd not Anfwer, till having gain'd a little Breath and fome fhort Quarter, he had an opportunity to bid the Waterman Row them to the *Spring-Gardens.* Upon this inftruction, the fpeed of their motion was redoubl'd, and beyond their expectation, they found themfelves at once refcu'd from their Amphibious Antagonifts, and juft ready to fet Foot again on Land. *Dorinda*

rinda very glad to be ſhut of her Scurrilous Companions, afforded *Panaretus*
very little trouble to help her out of the
Boat, tripping up the Stairs with the
utmoſt Agility, and ſhowing in all her
Actions, a readineſs to attend her Spark,
where e'er he'd carry her. *Panaretus*
having diſcharg'd their Old Badge and
Jacket, immediately directed their Steps,
and ſoon arriv'd to the Place aſſign'd
for their Recreation.

At their entrance, being attended
by the Menials of the Place, with their
uſual Diligence ; upon *Panaretus's* Requeſt, they were conducted by them to
an Agreeable Arbor, where the whiſ-
pers of the Ambient Air, joyn'd with
the ſweeter Harmony of Chanting
Birds, gave them a moſt engaging
Welcome. Nothing that the moſt
enlarg'd Fancy cou'd form, and Teeming Deſire wiſh for, was here
wanting ; its retir'd Incloſure, and
every winning Beauty of Fertile
Nature, ſeem'd to Conſpire with a ſort
of induſtrious Emulation, to add a freſh

Gult

Guſt to their Felicity.   The fragrant Roſe, the verdant Graſs, and all the dazling Glories of a blooming Spring, entertain'd their every Senſe, and left nothing wanting, that the moſt fruitful Nature, yet more refin'd by Elaborate Art, cou'd produce to give them freſh Delight.   Their Receſs being thus Decorouſly adapted to their deſires, and their Table plentifully (I need not tell you dearly) furniſh'd with the beſt Accommodations of the Houſe: After *Dorinda* had by Recounting ſome of the preceeding Circumſtances of their Affairs, put *Panaretas* to a Neceſſity of making his Acknowledgments for the preference ſhe had given him : She took occaſion, with an Air ſeemingly Accidental, to ask him "Whether "ſhe was the firſt ever had the Hap-"pineſs of gaining his Affections? The Homeneſs of this Queſtion, ſo unexpectedly put to him, caus'd a viſible Alteration in his Countenance, upon which taking advantage, ſhe importunately preſs'd him Ingenuouſly to con-
                                                        feſs

fess " Whether some Lady had not really
" been before her ? *Panaretus* wou'd
very fain have Eluded this, but finding it impossible to put it off, with some
Hesitation confess'd, " He had some
" light Thoughts of that Nature once,
" but finding Ungrateful Returns, soon
" quitted all Solicitude concerning it.
Dorinda having pull'd her Point so far,
was resolv'd not to let him rest, till she
had made him Recount the particulars
himself, of his Amour with *Cælia*; but
so artfully manag'd the matter, as fully
to quit her self of her Promise to *Phylastratus*, by giving him no Room to
mistrust she knew any thing of the matter before. *Panaretus* finding no possibility of avoiding displeasing her, without complying with her Request: After he had acquainted her how Ungrateful the Task she had set him, was
to him, proceeded to give his Narative as follows,

THE
AMOURS
OF
Panaretus and *Cælia.*

NO fooner had I pafs'd through the ufual Levities of Childhood, and arriv'd juſt to the Buddings of Reafon, but I found my Breaft imprefs'd with the moſt unaccountable Diforder, and ſtrangeſt Emotions, it ever had before experienc'd. The native Brifknefs of my Temper, and Eafinefs of my Mind, was I know not how, ſo all on a ſudden ruffl'd and confus'd, that I cou'd ſcarce perſuade my ſelf I was the fame Perſon. Long was it, before the ſlender Stock of Reflection I was then Maſter of, cou'd Suggeſt the Cauſe of this alteration; For tho' I every Day experienc'd my Inclinations altogether E-
ſtrang'd

ſtrang'd from their wonted Bent, and
all the Diverſions which us'd moſt ſenſibly to delight my Fancy, appear'd dull
and inſipid : Yet it was a conſiderable
time before I cou'd any ways account
for the difference. Love was a thing,
as yet my Breaſt had not been Suſcepti-
ble of ; Its true, I had learn'd to Form
the Verb *Amo*, through all its Moods
and Tenſes, and knew likewiſe the
difference between *Oſculor te*, and *Oſculor a te* : But yet, I never thought
my ſelf any further concern'd in any of
theſe things, than as they were a part
of my Exerciſe. *Virgil* and *Ovid*, I
was ſenſible made a mighty Splutter a-
bout ſuch Stories, but they were Gentlemen whoſe Company I'd part with at
any Time, for a Game at Tag, or
Hoop and Hide. But time, and the repeated inquietude of my Breaſt, at laſt
made me too ſenſible I had Contracted
a Paſſion which was not eaſily to be
diſcharg'd ; The Vicinity of my Fathers
Abode to that of *Calia's* ſo often afreſh
reviv'd my diſturbance, that I cou'd

H 4   not

not always be ignorant she was the
Cause of it. Every Day gave me new
Convictions, and tho' at first, I cou'd
easily have imagin'd the Commotion in
my Bosom, was owing to any thing
sooner than Love : Yet at length I
cou'd not but know, that that, and
that only, was my Malady. Being thus
(by an anxious Reflection on the Circumstances of things) fully convinc'd
that my Play-Fellow *Cælia*, (for that
she had been from my Infancy) had
insensibly got the Ascendant over my
Heart: I immediately found even the
little Reason I then possess'd, highly
Condemn'd and disapprov'd of my
Passion. Notwithstanding the tender-
ness of my Years, seem'd to lay me o-
pen as an easy Prey, to any Assault of
this Nature : Yet, by I know not what
Impulse, I had a Thousand boding
Fears incessantly wrack'd my Soul. I
know not how it was, but in spight of
all those dazling Forms, my eager Passions, wou'd force my Fancy to dress
her up in, I still cou'd not but entertain

tain some Thoughts she wou'd not Merit my Love. Do what I cou'd, my
Understanding wou'd be arguing against
me, and tho' the hurry of my Passions
was so great, that they seem'd above
controul, yet sometimes it wou'd re-
sume its Power to check them. I found
it impossible to be Sedate, and have a
good Thought on her ; there was something whisper'd she wou'd prove Ungrateful, Insolent, Unmannerly, &c.
and least that shou'd not be thought
a Disuasive strong enough, wou'd further suggest, she really now was Mo-
rose, Fickle, or Unpolish'd at best.
But yet so strangely impetuous, and
irresistable was my Passion, that it bore
down all Obstacles, and by mere Violence drove my Will to form a Resolution that shou'd consist with its Gra-
tification.

Youth, Passion and Folly, having
thus bore down the more sage Resolves
of Reason : I wholly gave my self up
to their violent Impulse, and having
by the nearness of my Residence to that

of hers, and her being so frequently before engag'd in my Company at the
agreeable Paftimes of *Hot-Cocles, One
and Thirty, Queftions and Commands,
&c.* all the eafinefs of accefs to her I
cou'd wifh for, by aukard Heffitations,
fheepifh Looks, and feveral other re-
diculous Intimations; gave her foon
fuch fhrewd hints, my Intentions went
further than was common to Play-Fel-
lows, as quickly fet her to Confult her
Mother, and Sifter, about my meaning, and what returns fhe fhou'd make
me. *Demogoga* and *Sycophanta* being
thus fully inform'd of my private proceedings with *Cælia,* prefently Collected
what the tendency of them might be:
And thereupon, immediately Documented their Young *Sycophanta* to carry
her felf in fuch a manner, as might fecure me entirely to her Intereft. Nothing of that innate Sullennefs, and ill
Nature which I afterwards found to
be infeparably united to the whole Family was then at all to be difcover'd;
but the fweeteft and moft obliging behaviour

haviour, fhe cou'd poffibly carry on, was ftrickly enjoyn'd her to be fhewn towards me; and indeed, fo well did fhe keep up to thefe inftructions for a confiderable time, that fhe abundantly feem'd to obviate, all that my Prophetic fears had fo ftrenuoufly urg'd againft her.

All things being thus adjufted for my carrying on my Amour with her, by frequently reforting to *Sycophanta* her Sifters Houfe, I foon had an opportunity of Communicating my Paffion to her, with the greateft eafe in the World; and therefore, taking the advantage when *Sycophanta* had left us alone together for that purpofe, with Confufion in my Face, and I know not what fort of damp and awe upon every Power of my Soul, I abruptly deliver'd what my affection fuggefted to me. At my firft Addreffing my felf to her, agreeable to her Inftructions, fhe feem'd under the greateft furprize in the World, and fuch an (as I then thought) agreeable Blufh overfpread her Face,

Face, as gave her new Beauties I had never before difcover'd; and after fome little recollection, fhe return'd the Offers I made in terms the moft Obliging and Kind, I really cou'd have hop'd for: Nay, I muft further ingenuoufly own, fhe carry'd her felf throughout the whole interview, with fuch an Air of Modeft deference and good Nature, as ftill aftonifhes me when I think on't. She was not above Sixteen when this pafs'd between us; an Age I thought knew no Obligations fuperior to thofe of Love, at leaft, was very diftant from the Arts of Deceit; but had it not been for you Madam, I had found my felf fatally miftaken.

The Subjects of this, and feveral following Meetings, were reciprocal Promifes of an inviolable Affection, till Time wou'd render it more convenient for us, to tye our felves yet more firmly, by *Hymens* Bands. Her Age being, as I before obferv'd, not above Sixteen, and my own advanc'd not much beyond it: Upon the confideration

tion of our Youth, and some other private Reasons, in which my Calling was
concern'd, I thought it convenient to
defer our Nuptials for about two Years.
Cælia, whose Part was now to be very
Complaisant, and good Natur'd, with
abundance of Readiness seem'd to ac-
quiesce in what I offer'd; pretending
her self entirely satisfy'd, both with the
Reasons I alledg'd, and the Time I allotted; pressing me further, very earnestly, not to make any body privy to
our Amour, but her Sister *Sycophanta,*
without whose Cognisance we cou'd
not possibly carry it on; to which, having immediately agreed, we went on
to consider of the Measures we shou'd
make use of in order to carry it on with
the utmost Secresie. Lovers, you are
sensible, Madam, seldom want any Instructions in this Case. For my Part,
(having got *Sycophanta's* Promise of
her utmost Assistance) I was very little
at a loss for Contrivances, and found
them answer'd with such a pleasing Success, for a Month or Six Weeks, that I
cou'd

cou'd not think my felf any thing lefs than a Candidate of the *Elifian-Fields.* For this Time I revell'd in all thofe pleafing Extravagancies, that Youth, and an eager Paffion cou'd prompt me to; continually repeated, with the moft vehement Ardour, the Teftimonies of my Affection, and as continually had them return'd in the fame manner; till being fully fecur'd from making a Relapfe to fober Reafon, my Defigning-Cabal thought fit to fufpend my *Fool's Paradife,* or at leaft give me a more fparing Allotment of it, the better to mould me to their Purpofe.

Calia having given a thorough Account, to even the minuteft Particulars of what had pafs'd privately between us; amongft other things that afforded them Matter of Confultation, the Propofal I had made of ftaying two Years, was what they cou'd by no means approve of. Delays of that kind, they imagin'd were dangerous; fomething or other might bring me to the exercife of common Senfe, and then all thofe

great

great Hopes they had of making me
the common Prey of the whole Family,
had all been utterly loſt. It was immediately reſolv'd therefore, that the preſent Fit of Fooliſhneſs they had then
ſcrew'd me up to, ſhou'd be improv'd
to ſuch advantage, as might make me
ſuperſede my preceeding Reſolution,
and quite mad to huddle up the Match.
The Reaſons I had given for declining
Marriage ſo long, were too ſolid to be
openly oppos'd ; and then it wou'd Have
ſpoil'd the Pageantry of Modeſty alſo,
if Mrs. *Cælia* was to appear forwarder
than I, and therefore it was eſteem'd a
more effectual way to give me ſo many
vexatious Interruptions in my Amour,
as might make me marry her in meer
Pet. For the better effecting this, *Cælia* was to be continually buzzing in
my Ears, her Deſire of keeping Matters ſecret; and *Sycophanta*, out of her
abundant Friendſhip to me, was to acquaint me with the reaſon why her Siſter expreſs'd ſo much Uneaſineſs for
fear of a Diſcovery; becauſe ſhou'd *De-
magoga*

magoga have the leaſt Intimations of what had paſs'd. Oh dear! ſhe'd be ſo very angry, ſhe'd never be pacify'd. In the Interim, the better to ſtrike an Awe on me, *Demogoga,* her ſelf, whenever I met her, was to make the obſequious Crouchings of the Coxcomb; the agreeable Returns of Sour Looks, and ill Manners. Having thus unanimouſly concerted their Meaſures, each prepar'd her ſelf to act the Part allotted, as Opportunity offer'd.

Mean while, I full of I know not what Romantick Notions of the Felicity I had, and was to enjoy; thought every thing that diverted my Imagination from running upon *Cælia,* an ungrateful Interruption of the moſt exalted Pleaſure of Humane Life: My Luxuriant Fancy painted her ſo extravagantly pleaſing to every Senſe, that I thought it cou'd never ſufficiently dilate upon her. Nay, ſo great was the Aſcendancy my Paſſion, or rather Folly had gain'd, that even my Reaſon ſeem'd to remit its former Sentence, and pronounce

nounce her worthy of my Affection. All my former Fears were now totally hufh'd and filenc'd, and fo far was I from being in any Pain of that Nature, that I imagin'd my Happinefs already fo confummate, as to be out of the reach of any Difappointment. To have entertain'd any Doubts of *Cælia*, had been a great deal worfe than Blafphemy; and to have pretended to compare her to any thing lefs than an Angel, the moft vile Detraction. I fhou'd aftonifh you, Madam, fhou'd I endeavour to recount never fo highly the exceeding Folly of my Thoughts; and therefore fhall content my felf with thus barely hinting them, and proceed in my Story.

Being thus fully flufh'd with the airy Conceit of the *Utopian* Happinefs I was poffefs'd of, I eagerly went on in my wild Facination, continually reforting, in my accuftom'd manner, to *Sycophan-t's* Houfe, and abandoning my felf of ill the reafonable Enjoyments of Life, wholly gave up my felf to the dull Expectations

pectations of feeing my Miftrefs. For now it was the Scene began to be ftrangely revers'd. *Cælia*, I'll warrant you, was as hard to be feen as the Emperor of *China*; and when, (by the Contemplation on *Patient Grizzle*, or fome other bright Example of Note, I had footh'd the Reftlefnefs of my Defires, to a Degree below Frenzy; for, really to be Ingenuous, that was all I cou'd boaft of) it was thought fit fhe fhou'd reward my two or three Hours waiting with her Perfonal Prefence: No fooner had fhe dandl'd her Fool out of his Pet, and tedioufly harangu'd me on the greatnefs of her Fear of her Mother's making a Difcovery, but I was again put to a frefh Exercife of my Patience. The violence of my Paffion, and Fondnefs of my Defires having made me wholly quit all other Company, the better to let flip no Opportunity of feeing her; by that means I every Day fpent, at leaft, two or three Hours to wait for her Company; never, certainly, was a more diligent Coxcomb known

known than I was, but all in vain, *Cælia* was not to be feen. Oh dear! fhe
was kept in very clofe; and as for *Sycophanta*, fhe, for her Part, was afraid
her Mother had fome Miftruft, and
therefore kept her in fo. But this was
not all neither, for when by waiting
two or three Days to no purpofe, they
had fpun my Patience out to its fineft
Thread, *Cælia* was detach'd to make
her Appearance, a little to footh my
Vexation: No fooner was fhe in my
Company, but fo full was fhe of her
pretended Fears, that even the leaft
Noife, tho' but the Jumping of a Cat,
was thought fufficient to put us to the
Start, and make us huddle to hide our
felves with the utmoft Confufion. It
wou'd really excite your Laughter, fhou'd
I recount to you the many little Tricks
they made ufe of to perplex and har-
rafs me; fo arfully had they manag'd
me, or rather, fo abandon'd was I by
common Senfe, that I know not any
thing in the World I ever fo much
car'd as *Demogoga*'s making a Difcovery;
her

her very Name was terrible to me, and
tho' my manacl'd Reaſon wou'd ofter
upbraid the Abjectneſs of my Fears
yet I found it impoſſible to quel them
It was full a Year before I entertain'd a
Thought of freeing my ſelf from ſo
vile a Slavery, when being quite wea
ried out, with that continu'd Series o
Diſappointment and Vexation they in
ceſſantly gave me, I reſolv'd my ſelf to
inform *Demogoga*, of the Affection I bore
to her Daughter. This Reſolution, Mrs
Cælia being firſt acquainted with, when
ſhe had ſhewn abundance of ſeeming
Reluctancy and Fear, was agreed to
and after She and *Sycophanta* had give
me ſome ſhrew'd Hints of what the
thought ſhe wou'd ſay to me, like
couragious Fellow, went about m
Task.

Having accordingly made my Ap
pearance, before our ſour Look'd Go
vernante, and gave her one of the be
Bows my Mother had learnt me, I wa
bid by her, with an Air between Gra
vity and Ill-Nature, to ſit down, whic
                                    bein

being done by me, she began very lear-
nedly to acquaint me, that her Room
was sad and dirty, and her Daughter
Celia was so concern'd it shou'd prove
so, she did not know what to do: "For,
added she, " the Child is a very good
'Housewife, and, cou'd she have her
'Will, wou'd be continually rubbing
'and scrubbing of Things over. The
ld *Trot* wou'd have gone on to gabble
er self out of breath, and me out of
'atience, with this, and such like im-
ertinent Cant upon her Daughter *Ce-
ia's* Industry, but I, (being quite tir'd
with the *Preface,* and not very well
pleas'd with the way she took to set
my Mrs. off) ventur'd so far to strain
Courtesie, as to interrupt her, telling
er, " Her Encomiums on Mrs. *Celia*
were altogether needless to me; the
great Opinion I had already conceiv'd
of her Merit, having abundantly anticipated all that cou'd be said of that
Nature; and, as an Evidence of it,
was then come to ask her Leave to
make my Addresses to her. My old
Termagent

Termagent being thus unexpectedly beaten out of her Road, and pusht home upon the Point, found her self at a great Loss how to answer me. The apparent Resolution I shew'd when I spoke, made her afraid she shou'd spoil all, shou'd she seem to decline my Request, and therefore, after she had humm'd and haw'd a considerable time, told me, " she was not wholly against my Re- " quest; but then her Daughter was " Young, a-lack-a-Day, very Young, " Poor Child! And so are you too, and " what can you do together so soon? " Do! answer'd I, why kiss one an- " other till we are fit to do something " else. And here I again urg'd the same Reasons to her very seriously, I had before offer'd to *Cælia,* for deferring our Wedding so long, desiring her further to consider of them, and if she did not esteem them sufficient, I wou'd act as she wou'd have me. *Demogoga* unable to oppose the Reasons I offer'd, seem'd wholly to concur with me, telling me she wou'd give me another meeting, and then

then would give me her full Resolution in the Interim, giving me full Li-
cence and Authority to kiſs her Daughter.

I need not tell you, I was now again
big with a thouſand extravagant Chy-
mera's, of I know not what ſort of un-
interrupted Felicity ; nor again trouble
you with an Account of the ridiculous
Vanity of my Thoughts upon this new
Scene of my Affairs ; for no ſooner had
the idle Figments gain'd poſſeſſion of
my Fancy, but I found my ſelf like the
ſimple Calf in the Epigram, vainly endeavouring to gather Nutriment from
the Teats of a painted Cow, and all the
mighty Hopes I'd conceiv'd, flamm'd
off with a Cloud inſtead of the God-
deſs. *Demogoga,* tho' ſhe could not a-
vow her Diſſent from the Reaſons I offer'd, for not conſummating my Nuptials immediately, yet cou'd not find
her ſelf eaſie to quit her firſt purpoſe,
of continuing to plague and diſappoint
me, till ſhe had merely fretted me into
a Compliance with her Deſires, beſides,

fides, by a peculiar Malignancy of Nature, fhe feem'd to delight and pride her felf in being Vexatious. There was no one Part of Life, fhe appear'd more eagerly to purfue, than that of endeavouring to blaft other People's Enjoyments; fomething in her had a fecret Pleafure in the Misfortunes of others, and fuch an inbred Venom attended every thing fhe was concern'd in, as render'd her One continu'd Plague, to all about her, worfe than *Egypt*'s Ten. If fhe might ever, in proper Senfe, be faid to be happy, 'twas only when fhe had fome way or other, contributed to the Mifery of others; the fight of her Neighbours Profperity, was a fure Confumption to her Bowels; and when fhe obferv'd the leaft Chearfulnefs in their Looks, it made her quite fick. That fhe might therefore make good, both her Purpofe and her Character, contrary to our preceeding Articles of Agreement, *Cælia* was order'd to abfent her felf, *Sycophanta* to put on her Mother's cloudy Looks, and fullen Behaviour

viour, and to treat me with all the Contempt and Indignities that Pride, back'd by Ignorance, and ill Nature cou'd poffibly offer, was the Part fhe referv'd in peculiar for her felf.

It is impoffible to exprefs the ftinging Regret it gave me, when I found them at the exercife of their feveral Parts. The morofs Carriage of *Sycophanta* towards me, when I enquir'd for her Sifter, at once fir'd my Soul with Rage and Difdain ; I cou'd not tell how to brook the Load of Injuries fhe daily accumulated on me. No Arguments wou'd be heard ; 'twas in vain to ask the reafon of their Proceedings. *Demogoga* thought fit to keep her Sifter out of my Company, and what was that to me ? Thus wou'd fhe infult even the moft modeft Remonftrances I cou'd poffibly make. Finding my felf thus even in the greateft Flufh of my Expectations, depriv'd of the darling Object of my Paffions, I knew not for what ; like a hungry Lyon that had loft his Prey, I feem'd to threaten deftructi-

I   on

on to all that came near me. A thoufand times I curs'd the Day that e'er my
Eyes fet fight on *Calia*'s Face; and tho'
I cou'd not perfuade my felf fhe was
any ways culpable of the leaft Falfhood
towards me; yet fo keen were my Refentments, and eager my Defires of being reveng'd on *Sycophanta* and *Demogoga*, that I began to entertain a fort
of Wifh, fhe might prove fo, that I
might have an Opportunity of venting
my Fury upon them. Never did greedy Mifer, in fpight of Gout, and Wi-
dow's Curfe, drudge with more inde-
fatigable Labour and Toil, to increafe
the bulk of his Soul-damning-Bags, than
I did to fee *Demogoga*; I hunted after
her Night and Day; trac'd all the fecret
Avenues, and fcandalous Conventions,
fhe us'd to refort to; but found it impoffible to get accefs to her. She flew me
like the Peftilence, and well fhe might,
for I think verily, had I light on her at
that time, I fhou'd have fpurn'd her
under my Feet; fo impetuous is the
Force

Force of an enrag'd and difappointed Lover's Refentments.

Our Cabal, (after having try'd Practices upon me in this manner for two or three Days) finding the Effect widely different from what they expected, began to think it dangerous to pufh things any further this way, leaft inftead of making me marry (as they wanted me) prefently, they fhou'd at laft put me into fuch a Ferment, as might extort a Refolution from me of never marrying, at leaft, not *Cælia* at all. *Demogoga* found that her infolent Ingratitude, in receding from our Agreement, was fo highly refented by me, that it render'd it very unfafe to continue the Practice any longer; and tho' it very much regretted their Pride, and natural Litigioufnefs of her Soul, any ways to oppofe what fhe had once purpos'd, yet found her felf at laft prevail'd on, to endeavour to reconcile me. And therefore 'twas unanimoufly determin'd, the next time I came to *Sycophanta*'s Houfe, *Cælia* fhould be dif

mifs'd

miss'd to me, and use all the little *Judas*'s Arts she cou'd think on, to still the impetuous Rage I was in, and flatter me again into a good Humour.

Accordingly, the next Time I was come, with my usual Rage and Indignation, to enquire for (or rather to surprize) *Demogoga* at *Sycophanta*'s House, the better to have vented my Resentments on her, *Cælia* having receiv'd Intelligence of my being there, immediately made her Appearance. When she came in, I was struck with the utmost Astonishment, my Heart was as 'twere overspread with such a convulsive Palpitation, as made me unable to speak for a great while; but my young *Parasite* observing the wild Distraction that hung over my Countenance, taking me by the Hand, proceeded so well to act up to her Instructions, as to bring the Fool, at last, out of his Dumps. Having thus, by her little Arts, brought me just into a Good-Humour enough to give her an *Audit*, she went on with an Air of abundance of seeming Concern,

to ask the Reaſon of the Indifference I
ſhow'd towards her; and when by way
of Rejoinder in the Agony of my Mind,
I vehemently declaim'd againſt her Mother and Siſter, for treating me as they
had done, and as is common to Minds
under the accute Senſe of Injuries, ex-
agerated every Circumſtance thereof;
with all the Sweetneſs of the moſt mo-
deſt Deference, ſhe ſeem'd to lament
their Rudeneſs towards me, earneſtly
entreating me to paſs it by for her ſake,
and not any more to perplex my ſelf
about them. I muſt confeſs, not-
withſtanding my Blood boil'd with
the Indignation which before had fir'd
my Breaſt; yet ſo moving was her Behaviour, ſo more than ever before ear-
neſt her Vows and Promiſes, and yet
more irreſiſtable her Tears, (which ſhe
had plentifully at her Command on this
Occaſion) that I found my ſelf wholly
unable any longer to retain my Reſentments. She ſeem'd ready to ſacrifice
every thing to my Pleaſure, and gave,
as I thought, ſo many endearing Proofs,

of

of an undiſſembl'd Affection, as left no
room for any doubt of her. I ſhou'd
quite tire you, ſhou'd I recount all the
remarkable Particulars of her Behaviour at this time. She afreſh repeated
all the preceeding Aſſurances ſhe had
given me, both by her Pen and
Tongue, of an entire and inviolable
Affection, told me, " That neither Mo-
" ther, Siſter, nor any other Conſidera-
" tion in the World, ſhou'd ſtand in
" Competition with me. And omitted nothing ſhe thought wou'd give me
ſatisfaction of her Conſtancy. For my
Part, tho' I was highly incens'd againſt
her Mother, and Siſter, yet I found it
no difficulty to think well of her; ſhe
was lodg'd too deeply in my Affection,
to need a long Apology in her Excuſe;
every Syllable ſhe ſaid therefore gain'd
an entire Belief from me, and I thereupon parted from her, with as ſure a
Confidence of her being entirely my
own, as if I had bound her faſt in
the Matrimonial-Nooſe.

It

It will no doubt very much furprize you Madam, if I tell you here ended the Amour of *Panaretus* and *Calia*, but the fatal experience I had like to have had of its truth, is fo far from being a Miftery to me, that I muft confefs, I cant yet eafily forget it. When this laft Loving Interview between *Calia* and I happen'd, (for fo it prov'd) I had carry'd on my Amour with her for about Year and a Half; and it having almoft from its very firft Commencement, been attended with fo many perplexing Circumftances, as render'd it a continu'd Series of Plague and Vexation to me, about a Quarter of a Year before I Communicated the whole Matter to my particular Friend *Phylaftratus*, in order to get his Advice, and affiftance about it, which he having promis'd me, from that time I gave him a thorough Account of all that happen'd; and foon after, by his acquainting me with the juft Affection he had conceiv'd for you Madam, we became mutual Confidents to each other.

Our

Our Affairs being in this prefent Poſture, Two or Three Days before I had ſpoke to *Demogoga*, (as you before heard) I re- ceiv'd your firſt Letter by the Hands of *Phylaſtratus*. Who having afterwards heard from me what Treatment I had, took a refolution immediately thereup- on, of trying whether *Cælia* was really fincere or no, towards me, and wanting no Opportunity of purfuing his Purpoſe, immediately pretended to make his Ad- dreſſes to her. The firſt time he had a ſuitable opportunity of ſpeaking to her in this Nature, was about Twenty Four Hours after ſhe had been with me, at which time, in about Half an Hour, he made ſuch an entire Conqueſt over my Miſtreſs, as quite ſhov'd me out of her good Graces. Having thus bobb'd me of my Dutcheſs, (as he has often told me) he expeſted, he preſently perfuaded her to Treat me in fuch a manner, as makes me Bluſh to think I ſhou'd ever entertain any thing like a Paſſion for her. There he recount- ed the particulars of her Carriage towards

wards him, when *Phylaſtratus* had by his Stratagem brought him into her Company, ſhowing the Copy of the Letter he Wrote to her, with all the other Parts which has been before related in their proper place.] Her Carriage continu'd, carry'd in its every Part ſomething ſo aſtoniſhingly audacious, and void of common Shame, that nothing but the being an immediate Spectator, can convey any Idea of it to the Mind : And indeed, her Actions ſo well ſpeak her Character, that to attempt to draw it any other way, wou'd be an undertaking that carries with it, the higheſt Impertinence. And when I conſider, I was ſo fooliſh once to Love her, it makes me abundantly the leſs fond of the Task.

Thus, Madam, I have diſplay'd to you the greateſt weakneſs I ever yet was Guilty of ; I doubt not, you will Eſteem it a Paſſion the moſt Violent, grounded upon the leaſt Judgment, you ever yet heard on : And I muſt be ſo Ingenuous to acknowledge, that I am not able to Aſſign one reaſonable Inducement

I 5

ducement to my Affection; had she
been possess'd of Riches, I shou'd be far
from urging it, but so wholly uncapa-
ble was she of making any Boasts of
that kind, that had I Marry'd her, I
must immediately have furnish'd her
my self even with Cloathes. In her Family she cou'd produce none above a
Mechanic, and that too of the most
Servile and Laborious sort. Her Education so mean, it scarcely rais'd her
to the Knowledge of common Civility; and tho' her own Vanity and Folly, had pretty well estbalish'd her Beauty in her own Opinion, yet I believe I
shall be the last that e're will make a
Panegyric on it. And so much may
serve for the Amours of *Panaretus* and
Calia.

I am very sensible Madam, your curiosity will naturally lead you to inquire how *Calia* carry'd her self after
her disappointment: And tho' I must
needs confess it the difficultest part of
my Narative, yet methinks, I shant
half acquit my self of my Task, if I
don't

don't at leaſt make ſome ſmall Eſſays of this Nature. Finding her ſelf then, in the hieght of her expeƈtations, treated by *Phylaſtratus* (whoſe generous Friend-ſhip diſplay'd on this occaſion, I can never ſufficiently acknowledge) and my ſelf, with that Juſt Contempt and Diſdain her Aƈtions Merited, inſtead of reflecting on what ſhe had done with even the common remorſe of de-teƈted Guilt, gave her ſelf wholly up, to all the little invidious Praƈtices of an inconſiderable peeviſh Malice, render'd yet more deſpicable by ſtupid Impu-dence, and ill Breeding. Tho' I cou'd not but with ſome emotion obſerve the wretched Ingratitude of her Soul : Yet when I ſaw the ſullen Sourneſs that ſo viſſibly hung over her whole Counte-nance ; I cou'd not but Smile at the in-nate Baſeneſs of her Nature. The ſilly Baggage endeavour'd to vent her Spleen in Methods ſo void of common Senſe, ſo meanly Rude and Mobbiſh, that when I conſider what an Opinion I once had of her, I am really aſham'd to mention them. She appear'd when ever I happen'd to see her, something so strangely ungain, and awkward, that for my Part, I know not what to compare her to, except that which the Learned call an Occult Quality. *Sycophanta* too put in for her share of Ill-Looks, but that which afforded the most diverting Scene of all was *Demogoga*; such a Malignant Spite, seem'd as 'twere to lurk under her Aspect, as gave such a rueful Air to it, that 'twou'd really prompt the Laughter of a Stoic to look on her. Envious People you know have always sore Eyes, and to tell you the Truth, Poor *Demogoga* is so terribly afflicted with them, she is not able to bear the sight of me. You wou'd really smile to see how she will huddle, without all manner of regard to her Corns, to avoid it. I must confess, indeed, I am a little cruel to her, because I scarce ever see her, but I smile in her Face, but yet I can sincerely alledge this in my Defence, that 'tis not the Effect of a premeditated Design to plague her,

her, but there is something so out of the way splenetick in her Phiz, that I find it impossible to look at her, and be serious. But I shall have an Opportunity, I hope, sometime or other, of letting you see them all, and then you'll have a juster Notion of them, than any I can give you, by the most elaborate Description, and therefore shall put a Period to this my long Story. This being all the Account that can be given by me, *PANARETUS*, Coxcomb in chief in the whole Affair.

Dorinda having given the most steady Attention to *Panaretus*, throughout the whole Course of his Story, (and found that elevated Pleasure which is peculiar to a Breast inflam'd with the most ardent Passion, in observing the several Emotions of his Breast bearing an agreeable Harmony with the Language of his Tongue) let him proceed to the End, without giving him the least Interruption. But now, at last, finding

finding his Silence, in reference to his Story, give her the Liberty of Speech, proceeded to divert both her self, and him, with several facetious Remarks upon the many odd Turns of his Narrative. " Is this, said she, the same *Calia* that " was the Subject of your P O E M? " Yes, Madam, answer'd he, the very " same; and the mischief on't is, even " *Licentia Poetica* won't bring me off, " and yet that, and Liberty of Con- " science, has justly been esteem'd to " quit all the Vilains, Fools and Flat- " terers in the Kingdom. Had she, " indeed, been some celebrated Jilt of " Quality, a few well-pen'd Lies, that " all the World is able to detect, might " have pass'd well enough for some of " the sublimest Flights of the Poet, e- " specially if he wanted a new Coat; " but to use so much Fustian, without " so much as the Hopes of a Dinner, " will ever be adjudg'd, by all that " have any Taste in Poetry, unworthy " of the Spirit of a Poet. Having mu-
tnally entertain'd each other with these
and

and such like chearful Reflections, after they had taken a Walk over all the
moſt pleaſing Parts of the Garden, the
Time drawing pretty near that *Panare-*
tus had promis'd *Phylaſtratus* to be in the
Mall; he propos'd the going there to
Dorinda, as the next Place of their Diverſion, to which ſhe very readily a-
greeing they immediately quitted the
Place, with the uſual Compliments,
from its Attendants, in order to take
Water to *Whitehall.*

Panaretus, the better to avoid being
again ſtunn'd by the Vociferous Ruſticks,
that in their wonted manner offer'd
themſelves, having quickly declar'd his
choice of One of them, was inſtantly
ſeated by him, with *Dorinda* in his Boat,
and with little or no Interruption in
their Paſſage, landed at *Whitehall*, according to deſire; whereupon immediately diſcharging him, they proſecuted
their Steps ſo as preſently to reach the
Mall. The Time making very near approaches, that was appointed for *Phy-*
laſtratus to be there, *Panaretus* endeavour'd

vour'd to divert her as well as he cou'd by directing her Eye to the several beautiful Marks of Magnificence, that all round them presented themselves to their View: They had not reciprocally entertain'd each other in this kind, above two or three Minutes, but, on a sudden, found their Ears assaulted with such an unaccountable, promiscuous Heap of Gabble, as made them have some Apprehensions the Confusion of *Babel* were again reviv'd, and that the angry Architects were ready to throw their Tools at each others Heads, for not being able to distinguish between *Bricks* and *Mortar.* The Variety and Eagerness with which the Sound was deliver'd, presently caus'd them to look behind them, from whence they perceiv'd it plainly to come, when immediately they found the Scene no less surprizing to their Eyes, than confounding to their Ears. Such a Heap of Gold and Silver Lace swallow'd up their whole Eye-sight, as left no room for any thing else but Wonder and Amazement. *Panaretus,*

naretus, for his Part, ſtood Gaping and
Staring, like a Country-Booby at a *Ra-
re-Show*, not able to imagine for a great
while what they were. Their Sheepiſh-
Looks, Antick-Shrugs, Creepeing-Gate,
and every other Symptom of a light
and inconſiderate Coxcomb, made him
preſently conclude their Cloaths the beſt
Thing they carry'd about them, but yet
he cou'd not conceive how they come
by them. Whilſt his Mind was fully
buſied with theſe, and ſuch like Reflections, he found himſelf yet more ſenſibly diverted by One of them's pulling
off his Hat, (with the moſt extravagant Geſtures and Grimace he ever yet
ſaw) to *Dorinda*, and upon her making
ſome indifferent Returns to the Ceremony, their all making their Approaches
with ſuch aukward ridiculous Cringes,
as wou'd be a real Diſgrace to a Mon-
key: Looking hereupon at her, and
obſerving her ſmile, he reſolv'd to ſtand
ſilently by, and ſee what they wou'd
do, which he had no ſooner done, but
they all began preſently to ſalute *Dorinda*,

da, with a, *Me be ver glad to delever you, Madam, from de Perfecuſhon of dis* Angliſh ; *de* Angliſh *be ver dull,* not fit to *walk by you ; dey no Aur, no Grace, me ſhow you,* &c. After which heap of bad *Engliſh,* and worſe *Impudence,* they of-fer'd to take her from him, at which *Dorinda* laughing very heartily, told him, " He muſt reſolve now to keep " his Miſtreſs by Knight-Errantry, or loſe her for ever. *Panaretus* ſeeing her rally him ſo merrily, and them ſo inſuf-ferably Inſolent, cou'd not tell what to think, whether they were in Jeſt or Ear-neſt he cou'd not tell how to brook the impudent Language they jobber'd con-cerning him, and therefore immediately drew his Sword telling them, " If they " did n't give him their Room he ſhou'd " make a Hole in ſome of their lac'd Coats. Brandiſhing his Rapier hereupon, and evidencing by the Intrepidity of his Countenance, that he was reſolv'd to make his Word good, wiſely conſi-dering the Matter, and finding, accord-ing to their A-la-mode Way of Compu tatio tation they were not an equal Match to him, wanting juſt Three of being Ten to One, they all inſtantly vaniſh'd like ſo many *Meteors* in the Air; Happy was he that cou'd run faſteſt; 'twas impoſſible for the quickeſt Eye to purſue them ſo faſt, but that it wou'd loſe Sight of them in a Minute. Finding himſelf thus entirely abandon'd by his *Antagoniſts*, almoſt in a Moment, the *Mall* at that time happening to have very few in it, he had a full Proſpect of them, from one End to the other of it, which he proſecuted with as much Earneſtneſs as if every thing as he had in the World had been carry'd along with them, but having, by the exceeding Swiftneſs with which they ran, preſently quitted the *Park*, and ſo got out of his Sight; he ſtood ſtill, Staring, and Gaping, as motionleſs as a Statue. *Dorinda* having laugh'd her ſelf quite Breathleſs, at the Oddneſs of the Adventure, ſeeing the Confuſion he was in, pulling him by the Sleeve ask'd him, " Whether he was 'aſleep? Aſleep! anſwer'd he, no. So

far

" far am I from it, that I think I have
" almoſt ſtar'd my Eyes out. Upon which
finding her again laugh very heartily,
" He ask'd her what ſhe laugh'd at?
" Laugh at! ſaid ſhe, to think how you
" were diſappointed in your *Heroes*,
" you're Miſtaken in them, you cou'd
" not have frighten'd them worſe, than
" by threatning to make a whole in
" their Coat; why there is not one of
" them has allow'd himſelf a Belly full
" this Two Years to get thoſe Cloaths,
" and you'd have gone and been ſuch
" a Wretch to 've made a hole in them
" the firſt Day. Fye *Panaretus*, thou
" art a ſtrange Vulgar Fellow I find, to
" think all that Gold and Silver Lace
" was made to Fight in, its well you're
" a dull Angliſh as they call'd you, elſe
" you wou'd not have been Ignorant
" they were made to Dance in. To
" Dance in! ſaid *Panaretus*, well then
" I think they Danc'd off. For my
" Part, I never ſaw Fellows run ſo faſt
" ſince I was born; and how much ſo-
" ever I might frighten them, I'm ſure
　　　　　　　　　　　　　" they

"they put me into a Bodily Fear, and
" had not *Dorinda* been the Matter in
" Conteſt, I ſhou'd certainly been be-
"fore hand with them in Running. I
" cou'd think of nothing but *Julius*
" *Cæſar*'s Fate, Two and Thirty Wounds
" at leaſt; if the Dogs wou'd have
" come to a Compoſition, I'd have given
" them a Leg with all my Heart. But
" Fortune, we truly ſay favours the
" Stout, and ſo I'm come of Tite and
" Sound. But Pray Madam, how came
" you to be ſo Couragious all along, do
" you know them? No ſaid ſhe, but I
" have often heard the Creatures Chara-
" &ter from ſeveral young Ladies of my
" Acquaintance, that frequently walk in
" this Place. Pray let me hear it then ſaid
" he, for their A&ions ſpeak it a very
" ſtrange one; ſince you have ſeen them
" anſwer'd ſhe, you cant reaſonably
" imagine any Deſcription of mine can
" ſpeak it better. All therefore, I at
" preſent requeſt of you is to put up
" your Sword, for had I not been very
" well aſſur'd, you'd have no occaſion
to

" to make ufe on't, I fhou'd never have
" been fo eafy under the drawing of it:
" If you took me for one of thofe ftrange
" Fighting fort of Creatures, call'd
" *Amazons*, you are far to feek in your
" Notions of me: Tho' to fee *Panaretus's*
" Courage is not at all unpleafing ; yet
" I muft confefs to 've feen his Blood,
" whatever Thoughts fome Romantic
" Ladies may have of that kind, wou'd
" have run me into Diftraction. *Pana-*
retus going to return her Complement,
found himfelf interrupted by fome Body
hitting him a little Clap on the Should-
er, upon which looking back, he found
himfelf and *Dorinda* accofted with a-
bundance of Ceremony by *Phylaftratus.*
The feeing him there, being before appointed was no furprize to him, tho'
his catching them fo pat without their
in the leaft perceiving him before, was
fomething beyond his Expectation : But
it was not fo to *Dorinda*, the fight o
him, put her in the utmoft Confufio
imaginable ; fuch a damp overfpread
her Spirits, that *Panaretus* had much a
d

do to keep her from Fainting in his Arms. *Phylaſtratus* obſerving the diſturbance his Preſence gave her, immediately proceeded to give a Reſolution to her Fears, in the moſt indulgent Expreſſions of a generous Pitty, by fully acquainting her with all that had paſs'd between *Panaretus* and him, in reference to her; the truth of which, being fully confirm'd by *Panaretus* himſelf: In a ſhort time, ſhe again reſum'd her preceeding briskneſs, and made her ſelf in the moſt moving Language of Gratitude, her acknowledgments to *Phylaſtratus* for his Generoſity. *Phylaſtratus* gave 'em the moſt obliging Returns, promiſing to omit no endeavours of being ſerviceable to them both, in reſpect to their Amour, and after having given them abundance of evidence of the ſincerity of his Intentions, told them " he deſign'd to ſecure " them for that Evening, adding fur-" ther, he was Maſter of ſome Tickets " of a Maſque that Night, and therefore was fully reſolv'd, they ſhou'd

Accompany

Accompany him thither; to which, very readily confenting, they directed
their Steps towards the *Hay-Market*
accordingly. On the way, *Panaretus*
entertain'd him with a full Account of
his whole Days Adventures, particularly the terrible Encounter he had
juft then with the *French* Men; at
which *Phylaftratus* laugh'd heartily,
telling him " he met them running as
" he came in the *Park*: The Place
" where I met them faid he, was the
" little narrow Alley, that comes into
" the *Park*, where they came all run-
" ning, as if they'd break their Necks,
" but feeing me in the paffage, fear-
" ing I fuppofe, a fecond Attacque if
" they joftled me, one of them very
" Couragioufly ventur'd to look back
" and finding no body purfu'd them
" gave the reft Intelligence, that they
" might flack their Speed, fo they brufh'd
" by me very quietly ; fo that after all
" tho' you did not actually make a hol
" in any of their Coats, yet the Cir
" cumftances of things render it fome
" thin

"thing probable, that their Breeches
" might suffer some damage on your
" account : This is certain, the Poor
" Fellows were in a pitious plight when
" I met them. Having thus mutually
diverted each other, by the accounts
they gave, they found themselves now
ready to enter the Theatre, which they
had no sooner done, but they found
that equally ready to entertain them.

The Matter of their Entertainment
was that inimitable Piece of Mr. *Congreve*'s, the Judgment of *Paris*. The
whole Performance was carry'd on in
every Part with such exalted Strains,
both in Numbers and Musick, as will
render it a continu'd Monument of that
unexampl'd Strength of *Genius* all concern'd in it were the happy Masters of
And in no Instance was the Three Goddesses contest more Famous, nor a juster
Subject for ancient *Bards*, than the excellent Competition between the Three
incomparable Masters, that lately set
it to Musick, will be to all intelligent
Posterity. The Beauties of Musick, as

K   well

well as Features, feem'd to defcend from Heaven, and appear'd to adminifter new matter for Conteft, which fhou'd moft fenfibly delight the Spectators; and even the Divinity of the Goddeffes, feem'd to receive frefh Beauties from the engaging Charms of their united Harmony. It were needlefs to tell you, that amongft the many others that this excellent Mafque inexpreffibly delighted, our prefent Company were fome: It feeming in every Part fo exactly adapted to their Pleafure, that even the minuteft Circumftances of it were not pafs'd over by them, without fome pleafing Reflections.

After the Diverfions of the Houfe were over, *Phylaftratus* wou'd take them home to his own Lodgings, where he had provided fuch a noble Collation for them, as abundantly evidenc'd, not only the endearing Regard he had towards them, but alfo the enlarg'd, and unbounded Generofity of his Nature. The regular Decorum, with which every thing was manag'd; being a ftrong In-
centive

centive to their Appetites, they all eat a
very plentiful Supper, and after proceeded to all those Diversions that are common among Friends on such Occasions:
Till the lateness of the Hour urging irresistable Reasons for their Parting; after they had reprocicably given each o-
ther all the endearing Assurances of a
strict and unalienable Friendship, they
cou'd possibly think on, *Panaretus* and
Dorinda took Coach, and parted with
him. After this, the speed with which
they were carry'd soon bringing them to
Dorinda's Door, *Panaretus* having conducted her in, after some short Endearments had pass'd mutually between
them, took his Leave of her, and then
immediately re-entring the Coach,
was upon his Order instantly drove to
his own Place of Abode.

Leaving now our happy Associates to
make their several Reflections upon the
present Posture of things, our Story now
requires some Account to be given of *Vulpone*, who soon after these things had been
transacted, return'd out of the Country,

and no sooner had got off the Aches which the Fatiegue of his Journey had produc'd, but he began to be very inquisitive with *Dorinda*, about *Phylastratus*, desiring to be fully acquainted with all the Particulars of his Carriage, since his Absence: In Answer to which, she told him, "She was able to give no "Account of him, that was any thing "new, his Behaviour being no ways "varied from what it was when he was "present. Upon this, the Old Gentleman took occasion, to tell her of his entire satisfaction of *Phylastratus's* Merits, earnestly pressing her to comply with his Suit, and prepare her self to receive him as a Husband. "You'll let him "ask me first I hope, answer'd she, for "tho' I am ready to acknowledge with "you, that *Phylastratus* is a very Wor- "thy Gentleman, yet I am fully per- "suaded, to Marry me, is the least of "his Thoughts, and I think verily a "little time will bring you to my Opi- "nion. Depend on't Sir, Men of his "Fortune and Sense, are not so apt to "fall

" fall in Love as you imagine. They
" Love to see the Vanity of the simple
" Girls, as they call us, and therefore
" they esteem our Company a tolerable
" Amusement for Half an Hour, that
" they know not how else to spend; but
" to be Ty'd for *Better for Worse*; is
" what frightens them in the bare sound.
Vulpone Chaff'd heartily to find his
Proposals so droll'd on by her, but finding himself unable to hold the Contest
with her, quitted the Room in a great
Pet.

He was no sooner gone, but she immediately set Pen to Paper, in order to
acquaint *Panaretus* with what had pass'd,
desiring him to bid *Phylastratus* by degrees so to deport himself, as to confirm the Account she had given of him,
adding, that she did not doubt turning his so doing very much to their
Advantage.

Panaretus having receiv'd these Instructions, took the first Opportunity
to Consult with his Friend *Phylastratus*
about them, and having to that pur-

K 3   pose

pofe fent for him as ufual, after a fhort Debate, they came to a Refolution as follows, *viz.*

That *Phylaftratus* fhou'd continue in appearance his Suit to *Dorinda*, as Vigorous as ever, and the better to keep Old *Vulpone* in the dark, fhou'd exprefs, in general Terms, a greater fatisfaction to him, in the Reception fhe gave him. This, tho' it feem'd in fome meafure to Clafh with the Propofals *Dorinda* had made, was thought to Adminifter more Room for carrying on their Scheme with the lefs Interruption. *Vulpone* being no ways likely to have any Miftruft of the Fallacy, when he exprefs'd himfelf fo unufually eafie: So that by this means, he cou'd have an Opportunity of bringing them together, with the greateft eafe in the World. Mightily pleas'd with the feafiblenefs of the Project, they further determin'd, to acquaint *Dorinda* with it, that fhe might Act agreeably, which *Phylaftratus* promifing to do very fuddenly; they put a Period to their Conference.

Do-

Dorinda being, accordingly, foon after fully inform'd of it, prefently fell in with the Project, promifing to omit nothing that was Conducive to the better carrying it on. And indeed, fo well was it manag'd by them all, for full a Quarter of Year together, that our Lovers feem'd to be wholly fwallow'd up in Delight. Under the Umbrage of *Phylaftratus,* they met together as often as they pleas'd, and Revell'd in all that abftracted Felicity which only Lovers can Form any Notion of. But Heaven having yet a Defign to exercife the Greatnefs of their Souls, by fome further Tryals, leaft they fhou'd be too much weaken'd, by a continu'd Courfe of foft Delights, fuffer'd fuch a Gloomy Cloud, to be all on a fudden fpread over their fhining Happinefs, as at once feem'd to unravel their whole Scheme, and blaft even the Hopes of future Enjoyments.

Notwithftanding by the affiftance of *Phylaftratus,* our Lovers had very frequent

Oppor-

Opportunities of Conversing with each other, yet such an unaccountable extravagancy of desire attended their Passion, as produc'd very fatal Effects. The many Opportunities they had of Communicating their Minds to each other when together, were not esteem'd sufficient, and therefore the Pen, as well as Tongue, was continually employ'd by them. By this means, *Dorinda*'s Pocket was constantly crowded full of *Panaretus*'s Letters, and happening one time to take some Snuff, that was stronger than ordinary, in her Unkles presence, she found her self oblig'd to pull her Handkerchief with greater Precipitation than usual out of her Pocket, with which she insensibly pull'd also one of *Panaretus*'s Letters, tumbling it upon the Ground. *Vulpone* observing the Passage, by a fatal Itch of Curiosity, was resolv'd by some Trick or other to get it into his Hand without her Knowledge, and thereupon, held her so earnestly in Discourse, as to get an opportunity to take it up with-

out

out her having the leaft fufpicion ; an l
being poffefs'd of it, immediately retir'd to perufe the Contents thereof.

No Language can here defcribe the
Rage and Fury that boil'd in *Vulpones*
Breaft at the perufal of it ; the fubject
of it happening to be fo Unhappy, as to
let him have a thorough light into the
whole Intrigue. To find himfelf thus
Egregioufly Cafhier'd of all thofe mighty
hopes he had conceiv'd of *Phylaftratus*,
nay, that even he himfelf was an Ac-
complice againft him, wrack'd his Soul
with fuch a peculiar Anguifh and Vexation, as only a difappointed Avarice
can fuftain. However he refolv'd as
much as poffible to diffemble his Difcontent, determining not to give *Dorinda* the leaft Hints of what he had difcover'd, but to go himfelf the next Day
to *Panaretus*, and give him fuch rough
Indications of his difapproving what
had pafs'd, as might give him fufficient
difcouragement not to proceed any further.

Agreeable next Day with Rag in his
K 5   Heart,

Heart, and Venom on his Tongue, he
went to a Tavern adjacent to *Pana-*
retus's Houſe and inſtantly ſent for him,
upon which immediately coming, after
ſome very ſhort (and hardly Civil)
Ceremonies, eſpecially on *Vulpone's* part,
had paſs'd, he immediately ſhow'd *Pa-*
naretus his Letter, thereupon, accoſting
him with all the ſurly Scurrilous Invectives he cou'd think on. *Panaretus*
exceedingly ſurpriz'd at what he ſhow'd
him, told him " He muſt Confeſs what
" he preſented to him was his own
" Writing, and if to Love his Niece was
" a Crime, he might be juſtly deem'd
" a Criminal. But withal modeſtly re-
monſtrated the Honourableneſs of his
Intentions, urging all that poſſibly
cou'd be ſaid in his Defence, except any
thing that might in the leaſt ſeem to
reflect upon *Dorinda.* But *Vulpone* was
deaf to all Arguments, nothing but an
inexorable Rage and Obſtinacy diſplay'd it ſelf in all he did and ſaid : He
ſtrickly prohibited *Panaretus* his Nieces
Company, adding Menaces to his Pro-
hibitions,

hibitions, and not so much as limiting
his expressions by common Civility. *Panaretus* told him " Did not the conside-
" ration of his Age, and being *Dorin-
" da's* Unkle put a restraint upon him,
" he wou'd certainly find (however Con-
" temptible he was pleas'd to expres
" himself concerning him) that he knew
" how to resent the want of Sense, as
" well as common Civility he had dis-
" play'd ; but since it was so, he might
" rest satisfy'd he shou'd be no further
" troubl'd with his Company, and
" therefore he need not give himself
" the Pains to bid his Servant shut the
" Door upon him, and thereupon Passi-
" onately quitted the Room, leaving
" Old *Gruff* to Chaw upon what he
" had said. But he having a Soul, that
was not to be impress'd with any thing,
but the cursed Desire of Money, very
little regarded the Violence of *Panaretus's* Resentments ; it did indeed afford him some Solicitude, when he
consider'd he was gone without paying so much as his share towards the
Pin

Pint of Wine he'd had, but when upon his defire, the Drawer refted fatisfy'd to take his Money off *Panaretus.*
next time he faw him, he trudg'd of very
chearfully, mightily pleafing himfelf
with the Thoughts of what he had done.

As for *Panaretus*, after in the Agony
of his Mind he had left *Vulpone,* with
the moft fenfible and ftinging regret of
Soul, he immediately directed his Steps
to a Young Gentleman of his Acquain-
tance, that having got a Commiffion,
was the next Day to go with his Company to *Holland.* When he was come
to him, giving him a general Account
of his having light on fome vexatious
Difappointments in fome Affairs he'd
been engag'd in, had taken a Refolution to Accompany him, for one Campaign. The Young Gentleman over-
joy'd at the Propofal, was very little
inquifitive into the Reafons he had, telling him he fhou'd fare as he did, adding further, he believ'd his Intereft was
fo great he cou'd get him a Commiffion, which afterwards he actually
perform'd

perform'd ; and having the next Morning a brisk Gale, they quickly found
themfelves in the Territories of the
States. Our Young Ramblers having
got themfelves a tolerable Lodging at
the *Hague Panaretus* began now to
think of acquainting, both his Father
and Miftrefs where he was, and calling for Pen and Ink Wrote to the Latter as follows, *viz.*

Thou Darling of my Soul,

*T*H E *Reafons I had to abandon both*
you and my Native Land, your Unkle
can acquaint you with, better than I ; I
wou'd only beg you not to afflict your felf
at it, but believe that Heaven (what ever
ill Aspect things may bear now) has a de-
fign to make me worthy of you even in
his Eye, who knows nothing Meritorious
but Riches: Doubt not, Lovely Maid,
but fome way or other, the Innocence of
our Love will be rewarded. I am now by
the Generous Friendfhip of a Young Gentle-
man plac'd at the Head of a Company,
and I am not in the leaft doubtful, but
the

the Thoughts of you will Inspire me so, as to act agreeable to my Character. This you may depend on, how distant soever my Body be from you; my Heart, my Soul, shall never be separated from you, but Bless you, even with their latest Breath: Believe me, thou lovely Innocence, I am, and ever will be, your entirely Affectionate Lover,

From the *Hague,* &c.   Panaretus,

The Place of my Abode here being so very uncertain, I can't no ways direct you how to send a Letter to me.

Having Wrote this, he enclos'd it up in another, to his Friend *Phylastratus,* in which he fully acquainted him with what had pass'd between him and *Vulpone,* desiring him to carry the enclos'd to *Dorinda* himself, and giving him all imaginable Assurances of the Continuation of his Friendship, put an end, for that time, to the Work, he had allotted to his Pen.

Leaving now our Young Hero to the eager Pursuit of that Glory, which is com-

common to aspiring and daring Spirits; the Course of our Story now, naturally, leads us to turn our Eyes to *Dorinda. Vulpone* had not in the least Communicated to her what he had done, but was contented privately to hug himself with the Thoughts, of his having been as Crafty as they were Cunning; by which means, she was not at all apprehensive of what had pass'd till about a Week after, when *Phylastratus* watching his Opportunity, when the Old *Chuff* was gone out, came and gave her *Panaretus's* Letter. No sooner had she Read it, but she immediately Sounded away, and when by the Care of *Phylastratus,* and her Maid, she was again brought to her self. So moving was her Complaints and piercing her Sighs. That 'twou'd have melted the most obdurate to have heard them. " Why, Passi-
" onately Cry'd she out, was I Born
" to endure a Grief so piercing, so un-
" equal to humane Nature! had his
" Cursed Avarice run him, to've
" rifl'd

" rifl'd me of all thofe Gifts of Fortune,
" my Parents with fuch Indulgent Care
" had laid up for me, Unhappy *Orphan*, I
" fhou'd hug'd and blefs'd my Poverty, if
" with it I cou'd have enjoy'd my beloved
" *Panaretus*, but to be depriv'd of him!
" This is to take my Fortune, my Life,
" and all that's dear away. *Phylaftra-*
tus did all that in him lay, to ftill the
tumultuous Hurry of her Paffions, but
all was fruitlefs, fo fenfibly was fhe
opprefs'd by her Misfortunes, that fhe'd
admit of no Confolation. Grief and
Sorrow took an entire poffeffion of her
Heart, and even the endeavour to Com-
fort her, gave a frefh addition to her
trouble. However, at laft, he perfuaded her to endeavour to hide her Difcontent, at leaft fo far, as not to let her
Unkle perceive it, and after having exprefs'd himfelf with the utmoft Tender-
nefs of a Compaffionate Pity towards
her; left her to footh the many Sorrows
of her Soul by foft Repofe.

After he was gone, *Dorinda* did indeed go to Bed, that her Unkle when

he

he came in, might not obferve the Diforder fhe was in, but as to Sleep fhe
was an utter Stranger to it; inftead of
that Calm hufher of all the Cares of
bufy Mortals, nothing but new Agra-
vations of her Miferies, and Defperate
refolutions of making fome Reprifals on
her Unkle, at any time cou'd gain Accefs to her Mind. Having thus pafs'd
away the tedious Hours of the Night,
about One a Clock fhe ftruck a Light,
and got up, after which, fhe immediately proceeded to Pack what Jewels,
and Money fhe had, in a little Cabinet,
defparately refolving to leave her Unkle,
and that Morning to take fome Stage-
Coach, and extravagantly follow the
wild dictates of her Blind Fortune ; a-
greeable, having fully Equip'd her felf
for the purpofe, between two and three
fhe Sally'd out unperceiv'd by any Body,
and directing her Steps to the firft Inn
fhe came at, happen'd to light on a
Coach that was juft then going out towards *Harwich*. It was indifferent to
her where fhe went, and therefore
                                    having

having upon enquiry found there was a sufficient vacancy in the Coach for her Reception, immediately agreed with the Coach-man to be one of his Passengers. Being Seated therefore with her fellow Traveller (which happen'd to be only one Young Lady) they instantly set out on their Journey. The Lady that was *Dorinda*'s fellow Traveller, was Wife to a Noble Man, whose Country Seat was ajacent to *Harwich*, and having receiv'd a Letter from her Lord, that requir'd her return into the Country something sooner than she expected, her own Coach not being ready to attend her, was forc'd to make use of the Stage-Coach, being to be met, however, on the Road by her own, towards the end of the Journey. This Lady having now by about half an Hour's Travelling with *Dorinda*, observ'd an exceeding Dejection hang over her Countenance, took the freedom, as is Common in such Cases, to ask her how she did? *Dorinda* whose Heart was now overwhelm'd with Grief, and

Eyes

Eyes brimful of Tears, being unable to make the Courtefy of her Requeſt, a-ny verbal Returns : The Lady eaſily collecting ſhe labour'd under the Preſ-ſure of ſome ſad Calamity, proceeded in all the winning Methods of Cour-teſy, and a generous good Nature, to endeavour all ſhe cou'd to get Intelli-gence of the Reaſons of her diſturbance; till *Dorinda*, unable any longer to con-tain the Impetuous Sorrows of her Soul, and won by the obliging Tenderneſs of her Carriage ; burſting out into a flood of Tears, gave her the whole Narrative of her Tranſactions. The Lady quite aſtoniſh'd at the many ſurprizing Par-ticulars of it, and the deſperateneſs of her Reſolutions, perſuaded her all, as in her lay, to return to her Unkle, but finding the Antipathy ſhe'd conceiv'd againſt him, impoſſible to be reconcil'd, ſhe Intreated her, ſince ſhe was reſolv'd to take up her Abode with Strangers, to let her Lord's Houſe be her Reſidence. *Dorinda* return'd the generous Hoſpi-tallity of her Offer, in the moſt endear-ing

ing Expreffions of Gratitude, fhe cou'd poffibly think on, modeftly declining the greatnefs of the Favour: But the Lady being too fenfibly mov'd at the Account of her Misfortunes, and Solicitous for her welfare, to be fo eafily put off, ftrenuoufly perfifted in her Requeft, and never left importuning of her, till fhe had comply'd therewith.

Dorinda's Breaft now was fo fully enflam'd with a Senfe of Gratitude, at the engaging good Nature of her fellow Pilgrim, that fhe thought her felf oblig'd as much as poffibly fhe cou'd, to relax the Trouble of her Mind, and fhow her felf at leaft a little Compos'd, in meer Complacence to her Benefactrefs. The penfive Air fhe before had put on, fhe fear'd might render her troublefome, and tho' the Grief fhe had Contracted, was too Potent to be eafily repell'd, even from her Looks; yet the Obligations fhe lay under to the Lady, feeming to render it neceffary, fhe induftrioufly hufh'd the Riot of her Paffions, and even forc'd a fort of Glimering Light
and

and Chearfulnefs on her Countenance.
The Lady finding fuch a happy change
in her Afpect, proceeded to tell her,
that fhe defign'd to make her Lord
believe, fhe was a Coufin of hers, that
was come with her to fee him, giving
her further, all the moft generous affurances of her Friendfhip, and her utmoft endeavours to engage likewife
the fame from her Lord.

Dorinda made her acknowledgments,
with that engaging fweetnefs of Modefty, and deference to her Quality, as
made her really delight to offer her frefh
Favours. She thought fhe cou'd never
enough exprefs the Efteem fhe had for
her; entreating her to take the freedom
of a Sifter with her, adding, That fhe
wou'd in nothing fo fenfibly Oblige her
as in doing fo. " Let Madam faid fhe,
" my Houfe, my Servants, every thing
" I have, be at your Command ; ufe
" them with as much freedom, as if
" they were your own. It wou'd take
too much room in thefe Papers, fully
to Recount the many Reciprocal endearments

dearments of their Converfe, there being nothing omitted on both Sides,
throughout the whole Courfe of their
Journey, that wou'd any ways conduce
to make them appear, every Minute,
more Lovely in the Eye of each other.

Having, by this time, run very nigh
the full Courfe of their Stage, they
were acquainted by the Coach-Man,
that the Lady's Coach and Six, now
made very near Approaches; whereupon they both began to prepare themfelves to go into it, and finding it accordingly come up to them, *Dorinda*,
and her Generous Fellow-Traveller,
immediately enter'd it, and in an Hour's
time after, found themfelves brought
to a happy Period of their Journey.

No fooner was the Lady enter'd her
Houfe, and welcom'd by her Lord, but
fhe immediately defir'd him to receive
Dorinda into his particular Efteem, telling him, as fhe had before determin'd,
that fhe was a young Coufin of her's,
whom fhe had brought down with her
for a Companion, and therefore defir'd
him

him to receive her as such. The Lord finding *Dorinda* so particularly recommended by his Lady, and observing the native Sweetness, and Beauty of her Mien, abundantly attractive of Respect, immediately receiv'd her with that obliging Courtesy, which the Account his Lady had given of her, and the inward Sense he immediately conceiv'd of her Merit, requir'd. But this did not content her noble Benefactoress, all the Servants in the House, from the Highest to the Lowest, were immediately call'd in by her, and strictly enjoin'd to pay the most obliging Deference to her, and immediately to fulfil her Desires, with as much Readiness and Freedom, as if 'twas she her self spoke to them. After this, entertaining her with a splended Banquet, she, her self, conducted her to a very fine Appartment, for her Lodging-Room, ordering her Gentlewoman to be her Bed-fellow. Mrs. *Betty*, (for so we'll venture to call her, tho', some no Doubt will heartily contend that there ought to be some Deference

between

between the Title of my Lady's Wo.
man, and that of every common Chamber. Maid) was very well pleas'd with
the Poft, her Lady had allotted her, and
tho', I can't fay, but a young Gentleman might have pleas'd her as well,
yet, the chearful Afpect, fhe difplay'd
upon this Occafion, fhow'd however,
fhe cou'd be a little pleas'd at the
Thoughts, even of a Female Bed-Fellow.

Every thing being thus generoufly
accommodated, both to the Ufe and
Pleafure of *Dorinda*, fhe found, (after
fhe had, about a Quarter of a Year, experienc'd the good Offices, the whole
Houfe feem'd to take Pride in doing towards her) the Edge of her Sorrows for
the Lofs of *Panaretus*, began a little to
wear off : Tho' the humble Modefty,
and fweet Affabillity of her Carriage,
made her belov'd by all about her, and
her Noble Benefactorefs, took no fmall
Pride in the Kin, fhe had adopted her
to : Yet, fuch a Secret Inquietude hung
over her Mind till now ; that however
pleafing

pleafing fhe might be to them; yet,
fhe found it impoffible to be fo to her
felf. *Panaretus* was not foon to be forgotten, and tho' Gratitude, and Civility requir'd her to difcharge her Countenance from all the Marks of Difcontent, yet fhe found it not fo eafy to quit
them from her Heart: But Time, and
the repeated Experiences fhe had had
of the peculiar Care, Heaven had hitherto taken of her; at laft, darting into
her Mind, the Repofe fhe ought, even
in Gratitude to put in Almighty. Goodnefs, fhe thereupon found her Mind immediately disburden'd of its preceeding
Load of Anxiety, and fuch fecret Springs
of Confolation, fenfibly dilate themfelves all over her Breaft, as gave her
fome Sort of glimering Forebodeings of
that Happinefs, Heaven yet defign'd her.

Now it was, fhe began to difplay a
Scene, that made all that faw her have
a fort of Doubt, whether fhe was not
fomething above Humane. The Match-
lefs Beauties of her Wit, and lovely Sweetnefs of her Temper, both render'd yez

L   more

more engaging, by a rais'd, and ingennuous Education, began a-frefh, to exert themfelves with that wonted Life and Vigor, as ever render'd her fo juftly admir'd by all that knew her. Amongft the many Others, that made too peering Obfervations of her Perfections, to retain the ufual Tranquility of their Minds; the young Lord of that rural Manfion, fhe refided in, and Husband to the Lady, we have often before mention'd, notwithftanding the Nuptial Obligations, he lay under to the Contrary, found himfelf too fenfibly imprefs'd by her feveral Beauties, to look on her without fome irregular Defires. Whether the natural Difpofition of his Blood, or the too often more prevalent Contagion, with Gentlemen of his rais'd Character, a Loofnefs in Principle, that bears down all the great, and everlafting Duties of Religion, as fit only to be exercis'd by the Mob, and fuch like contemptible Tools of defigning Priefts; whether either, or both of thefe concurr'd, is not an Enquiry we
                                    fhall

ſhall at preſent make; but that he
was not over Induſtrious to curb the
Ignoble (for ſo I muſt call them) Emotions of this Kind, the Event abundantly ſhews.

Dorinda happening one time to be retir'd to a very recluſe Part of the Garden, and ſpy'd there, by her Laſcivious
Admirer, immediately found her inno-
cent Solitude interrupted by the unexpected appearance of *Phylopones*, (for ſo
we'll call our young Lord for the future)
who after ſome ſhort Salutations, came
and ſat down by her. Very ſhort was
the Converſe held with her, before
(being quite enflam'd by the new cre-
ated Charms her Bluſhes gave her) he
began with all the couchant Fawning
of a mean and abject Luſt, to tempt
her Vertue. *Dorinda*, ſtruck with the
utmoſt Horror and Aſtoniſhment at
what he ſaid, told him, " She thought
" he had had a better Opinion of her,
" than to think ſhe cou'd bear to hear
" ſuch Language. No, my Lord, ſaid
ſhe, with a noble Diſdain and Indig-

nation

nation in her Looks, " I fpurn the very
" Thoughts of what you offer, and fome-
" thing fo much above a Woman's Rage
" has fir'd my Soul, that in fpight of
" the Obligations you have laid upon
" me, methinks I cou'd give their Au-
" thor the fame Treatment. *Phylopones*,
feeing the Violence of her Refentments,
thinking fhe affected to appear Drama-
tic, told her, " He muft confefs, what
" fhe faid wou'd found very Grace-
" ful from Mifs *Santlow*, on the Stage,
" but every body knew, behind the
" Scenes the Story was quite turn'd;
" and the fmug young Fellows that
" there ftood upon the Dodg for her,
" found it no difficult Task to convert
" the Romantic Notions of the Maid
" in the Mill, into the warm Careffes
" of a Nymph that has too much Beau-
" ty, as well as Senfe, to facrifice all
" thofe exalted Pleafures, that are fo in-
" duftrioufly accumulated on her, to
" the poor Lectures of a Parcel of old
" envious Priefts, who are themfelves
" paft the Tafte of them. See, Ma-
" dam,

" dam, the pretty Freedoms the little
" chirping Birds around us take ; they
" bill, and quench each others amo-
" rous Fires, without any of thofe idle
" Fears, which you amufe your felf
" withal, and feem, by their after war-
" bling Notes, to triumph o'er the
" groundlefs Superftition of us, (for
" whofe Pleafure they were made) in
" being more Timorous than they.
" Come then, Madam, ceafe thefe irk-
" fome Thoughts ; this pleafing Recefs
" feems purely made for Love, and the
" gentle *Zephyrs*, that all about us con-
" vey their winning Whifpers through
" the trembling Boughs, like the Voices
" of fo many *Cupids*, prefs you to make
" both me and your felf happy. You
" can't, you fhan't deny, fear not thou
" lovely Nymph, we're all alone-- Alone,
" indeed, (anfwer'd *Dorinda*, interrupting him) " when fo fatally abandon'd,
" by Vertue and Honour. To laugh,
" my Lord, is eafie, very eafie, 'tis what
" we Women can do, as well as the beft
" Free-Thinker of you all ; but, fure,

L 3   " bare

" bare Laughing will never alter the
" Nature of Good and Evil; if we do
" believe fuch a Thing as a Heaven to
" reward Vertue, and a Hell, as the
" fatal End of Vice; if we do believe
" an All-wife, as well as an Almighty
" Judge, takes cognizance of every
" Action of our Life, and this, (how-
" ever Intelligent of late the Age is
" grown) fome do, (at leaft profefs
" to) believe; furely you cannot think
" thefe are Notions, (were they ground-
" lefs) that are to be jefted out of the
" World? Why then, is that boafted
" Reafon, which fuch Gentlemen as
" you particularly glory in, wholly o-
" mitted, and nothing but that vagrant
" Levity made ufe on, even to debauch
" a Young, a Fencelefs Girl, as wou'd
" make its very Authors blufh, fhould
" they ever recollect it? This is a Pra-
" ctice fo common, that I can't but
" have fome Emotion when I think
" on't. 'Tis not only my particular Cafe,
" but what, my whole Sex have rea-
" fon to complain of: No fooner has
" our

" our Stature, (rather than Reafon)
" advanc'd our Defires above thofe Tri-
" fles that us'd to delight our Infant-
" Years, and the fatal Flatteries of all
" about us, puff'd our eafie unthinking
" Minds, with the vain Opinion of our
" own Perfections; but the fpoil of our
" tender Innocence immediately com-
" mences the Bufinefs of fome villanous
" Debauch.   No Arts, no Snares, no
" Toils, are thought too much, to effect
" our Ruin; and when our artlefs Youth,
" at laft, is fall'n their Victim, and the
" repeated Sacrifices we have made, both
" of our Virtue and Honour, have errac'd
" all Senfe of Guilt and Shame out of
" our Minds; the black, the hedious
" Terms of reproach you treat the eafie
" Proftitutes withal ; at once proclaim
" the wretched Condition of the Mif-
" creants, and the curfed Ingratitude
" and Treachery of thofe that firft fe-
" duc'd them. Is not this barbarous,
" My Lord ! Can Villany, fo black as
" this, become a Gentleman? Did Hea-
" ven give you that fuperior Power of

L 4

" Reafon,

" Reafon, the want of which you fo
" pride your felves in upbraiding us of,
" purely to make us with the more
" eafe your Sacrifice? No more, for
" Shame, infult us for being the Caufe
" of the lofs of Primitive Innocence:
" Let your *Miltons* and *Bickerftaff*'s, now
" employ their fine fpun Wits in exa-
" gerating the fad Reprizals your Sex
" has fince made on us: Let them now
" paint the Bafenefs; the Villany of
" your Proceedings with us; fet forth,
" in lively Colours, our tender Inno-
" cence attack'd with all the Hellifh-
" Arts of the moft experienc'd Debau-
" chery; and, above all, not forget to
" difplay the Names you give us, when
" you have gain'd your Ends. Were
" this done, my Lord, the World would
" fee fuch a Scene of Villany, Trea-
" chery, Ingratitude, and all that's
" black and hateful, as wou'd ftrike it
" with Horror and Amazement.

   Phylopones, at once, ftung to the very
Soul with the Force of her Reafonings,
and charm'd with the bright Afcendancy
of

of her Wit, found himself unable, a-
ny longer, to retain the leaft Thoughts
of offering any Violence to her Chaftity.
That noble Intrepidity of Soul, and
unfhaken Vertue fhe difplay'd in every
Word fhe faid, ftruck fuch a fecret
Awe on his Spirits, and damp on the
irregular Ebulitions of his Blood, as a-
bundantly guarded her from thofe In-
decencies, the Reclufenefs of the Place
where they where, might otherwife
have encourag'd him to have affaulted
her with. But yet, by I know not
what uncouth, modern Notions of Gallantry, he thought it a Reflection upon
his Wit, to appear baffl'd; though he
cou'd have been contented well enough
to defift any further Outrages; yet by
his Silence tamely to own himfelf in
the wrong, was what he thought was
by no means compatible with that di-
ftinguifhing Senfe, Gentlemen of his
Character are always put up for. To
be forc'd, at leaft, tacitly to confefs, all
the darling, as well as fafhionable Principles of our Gentry, (who have taken

fuch

such abundant Pains to refine our dull obsolete Notions, and made Religion the most easiest moderatest Thing in the World, so far from that ancient Ruggedness, as was wont to make every Thing else stoop to it, that rather than it shall give you any Disgust by what the Priests call, *earnestly contending for the Faith*, even *Mahomet*, or what you will shall be reconcil'd to it.) To be forc'd, I say, to seem to own all these fine spun Systems, carry'd as much of the Villain as the Sceptic in 'em, was what he cou'd not yet bring himself to; rallying therefore his scatter'd Forces together as well as possibly he cou'd, he resolv'd once again to endeavour to bear down his as yet too potent Antagonist. " Really, Madam, (therefore
" return'd he) you rail with the most
" Judgment I ever heard in my Life;
' and but that you know there is some-
" thing in your Face, that renders it
" impossible for one to be angry with
" you, you wou'd not, you cou'd not
" talk at this sad rate. For my Part,
                                    " was

" was I not to look on you, methinks
" I cou'd be terrible stout against you,
" but to encounter your Tongue and
" Eyes too, is, indeed, above my Match.
" Why you're ten times worse than
" *Sylvia*'s *Revenge :* Prithee, Child, have
" more mercy on us ; for tho', it must
" be confess'd, we Men are, some of
" us, sad Fellows, yet I wou'd venture
" to be sworn, there is not One in
" *England* wou'd give you half the ill
" Words you have given them; such
" sour Notions as these, believe me,
" will quite spoil your pretty Face;
" your frowning so will anticipate old
" Age, and fix the Hag upon your Coun-
" tenance, before you're Twenty. Did
" you ever see a Witch? No, my Lord,
answer'd she, " but I've seen several
" that have been bewitched, and that
" too with the most trifling inconside-
" rable Vanity that e'er infected Hu-
" mane Nature: And now I find by
" your way of expressing your self, you
" think me touch'd with it, I can't for-
" bear taking this Opportunity of letting
" you

" you fee all Women are not fo weak-
" ly vain.   Not but I muft freely own
" even the moft infignificant Levity in
" the World, under the Management
" of One of your Lordfhip's enlarg'd
" Wit, and fublime Education, may
" prove too forcible a Temptation to
" be eafily withftood, by fome unthink-
" ing Girls, who were before altoge-
" ther unacquainted with the Practice:
" But to fee fome of my Sex fo weak
" to be giggl'd out of their Vertue and
" Honour, by a Parcel of infipid Cox-
" combs, (who Ape you in fuch an
" aukward, uncouth manner, as wou'd
" at once make you fmile and blufh to
" fee them) to fee them, I fay fo mon-
" ftruoufly Foolifh, to take any notice,
" of fuch filly Soul'd Creatures as thefe,
" makes me out of all Patience. When
" ever I think on them, they put me
" in mind of the fam'd Bird at *Athens,*
" faid to be all Face and Feathers; and
" I am fully perfuaded, fo exact is the
" Similitude between them, that were
" it poffible to take away their Impu-
                              " dence

" dence and fine Cloaths, 'twould in-
" evitably reduce their very Eſſence to
" its primitive *Nihil.* Oh, Fie upon
" you! (cry'd *Phylopones*) you talk ſo
" wickedly now, I don't know how to
" bear you: A pretty young Lady, as
" you are, and not like the *Beaux*;
" Come, come, Madam, in ſhort, you
" want to be better documented; not
" love ſuch a pretty ſoft tender young
" Rogue as a *Beau!* I don't hate him,
" my Lord, (ſaid ſhe) and becauſe you
" ſhan't think me worſe than I really
" am, I'll readily acknowledge all that's
" valuable in him I like well enough;
" the Lace on his Coat, I'm apt to think,
" I cou'd put to a hundred pretty uſes;
" the Coat it ſelf, I confeſs, is general-
" ly very well made, tho' if 'twere
" patch'd, 'twou'd certainly ſuit him
" much better; and, in ſhort, cou'd I
" perſuade my ſelf, his Head is of half
" the value of his Perruque, I allow
" him to be one of the fineſt Creatures
" in the World.

No

No fooner had *Dorinda* fpoke thefe Words, but they found themfelves interrupted by one of the Servant's approaching to acquaint them that Supper, and his Lady, waited for them; whereupon, immediately quitting the Place, fhe was prefently follow'd by *Phylopones.*

After Supper, and fome little Merriments had pafs, each prepar'd to retire to their ufual Repofe. As for *Dorinda,* fhe found very little difficulty in getting foundly afleep; the whifpering *Euges* of her own Innocence, and the Opinion fhe had, that whatever *Phylopones*'s Defign was, by his late Proceedings, (whether to try her Vertue, or gratifie his own vile Defires) it was now wholly ceas'd, fo fully flatter'd her with a thorough Security, that fhe fhou'd be no further fubjected to any more Affaults of this kind, as quitted her Breaft entirely of all Solicitude about the Matter. But 'twas not fo with *Phylopones.* The feveral engaging Beauties of her Perfon, and lovely Delicacies of her Wit,

Wit, afresh reviv'd the irregular Emotions of his Lust: Every Reflection he made, upon what had pass'd between them, gave new Ferment to his Blood; and so far was the noble Opposition she made, esteem'd sufficient to awe him for the future, that it only stirr'd up in him the base Resolution of being more Vigorous in his Attacks. Nothing but the firmest Purposes to debauch her, cou'd gain the least admittance into his Mind; and so impetuously raging was his Lust, that he determin'd to omit no Opportunity of effecting his Design.

His incessant Vigilance hereupon, and her being altogether unapprehensive of his Intentions, soon presented the luscious Scene, of her all alone in her Chamber, to his lascivious Eyes. The sight of her under these Circumstances, made him impatient of all restraint, rushing therefore eagerly upon her, without any further Salutation, he caught her fast in his Arms, pressing her blushing Cheeks with innumerable Kisses, and offering

every

every other Violence and Indecency,
that an infolent and ungovern'd Luft
cou'd prompt him to.

Dorinda, quite breathlefs with ftrug-
ling againft him, and frighten'd almoft
to Diftraction, at the unexpected Extravagancy of his Proceedings, finding
her Strength not equal to carry on the
Conteft, in that violent manner, told
him, with the utmoft Rage and Difdain in her Looks, "If he did not im-
"mediately defift his bafe and unge-
"nerous Carriage, fhe wou'd alarm the
"Houfe, and, amongft others, his fo
"unworthily injur'd Lady to her Affi-
"ftance. *Phylopones* obferving too noble an Indignation difplay it felf in *Do-*
rinda's Countenance, any longer to hope
to carry her by Violence, inftantly quitted his hold of her, and abjectly. pro-
ftrating himfelf before her, us'd all the
little mean Arts, the vile diforder of
his Blood cou'd poffibly furnifh him
with, to tempt her to comply with his
Defires. He left nothing unfaid that
he thought wou'd any ways allure her,
telling

telling her, " The Love he bore to her
" was fuch, 'twas impoffible for him
" to live and not enjoy her. Love me,
" my Lord, faid fhe, 'tis falfe, you
" don't, you cannot love me; for if you
" did, you'd fcorn to tempt my Vertue.
" Love! Is a pure, a Heav'n-born Paf-
" fion, it can never, therefore, be the
" Parent of Two fuch hateful Crimes,
" as *Adultery* and *Ingratitude.* Confi-
" der, confider ferioufly, my Lord, how
" you will curfe, curfe from the very
" bottom of your Soul, that Tinfel-
" Beauty, you now fo much applaud,
" when in your cool and fober Reafon
" you reflect, 'twas that, that was the
" means to load your Noble Soul with a
" Guilt you never can fufficiently be-
" wail. Guilt! (anfwer'd he) What
" Guilt can there be, when Charms
" Ætherial prompt the Paffion? Did
" Heaven give us Appetites only to be
" reftrain'd? Impoffible! They that tell
" you fo, themfelves don't believe it.
" Heaven bids increafe, and to fuppofe
" it denies the Means of doing fo, is
" to

" to reverſe its own Decree. The Crimes
" you fear then, are nothing but the Fig-
" ments of a melancholly Brain, which,
" wou'd you once have Courage to
" ſhake off, and taſte the Bliſs is offer'd
" you, you'd leave them with as much
" Pleaſure, as you firſt receiv'd them
" with groundleſs Fear. A Genius like
" yours, ſhou'd ſcorn to be hagg'd with
" the idle Superſtition of the Mob, this
" wou'd be to extend the Terror of thoſe
" Bugbears, you are ſo frighten'd with,
" further than their firſt Inventors de-
" ſign'd them, and make that, which
" like the Story of *Raw-head* and *Bloody-*
" *bones,* was intended only to ſcare Fools
" and Children, a means to pall the En-
" joyments of the moſt rais'd Capaci-
" ties. Come then, and let us wanton
" our Hours away in ſuch ſoft De-
" lights, as only Beauty like, yours,
" can give : Let us be as free as Air,
" and unconfin'd as Thought, and
" ſcorn to abridge our ſelves of thoſe
" Pleaſures, which the Vulgar there-
" fore

" fore fear, becaufe they don't under-
" ftand them.

Dorinda finding he attaqu'd not only
her Vertue, but the noble Principles
with which 'twas guarded, began to
think her felf oblig'd to anfwer him,
not only in defence of her Perfon, but
of Religion in general; and was the
rather induc'd thereto, becaufe fhe obferv'd him fhew fomething like Triumph in his Countenance at his Performance. Fixing therefore, at once, that
Majefty and Sweetnefs on her Afpect,
which only a Mind unfhaken and inno-
cent can difplay, with all the Eafinefs
and Freedom in the World, gave his
labour'd Harangue the following Returns. " How witty are we, (faid fhe)
" in diffembling the inward Senfe of our
" own Minds; and fo fatal is the Preju-
" dice our Lufts put upon our Judg-
" ments, that there is nothing fo mon-
" ftrous, they can't perfuade us to em-
" brace. We Women, I confefs, my
" Lord, are very unfit to engage in the
" elaborate Subtilties of Polemicks; we
"have

" have no Schools, no Academies, to
" polifh, even that little Reafon we
" poffefs, no Learning is beftow'd on us,
" but what comes from Fellows who
" have no Notions of any Senfe, but
" what lies in the Heels, and there-
" fore engage on very unequal Terms,
" whenever we venture to oppofe fuch
" Gentlemen as you. But yet, your
" Lordfhip, methinks, has now ex-
" prefs'd your felf fo widely diftant,
" from what I cou'd not but ever think
" the Refolves of the fober Reafon of all
" Mankind, that I can't pafs by this
" Opportunity of fhowing my Diffent
" from you. That Ingratitude, the
" blackeft; the moft hateful that ever
" Wretch was guilty of, and that yet,
" if poffible, deeper dy'd by Adultery,
" fhou'd be mention'd by your Lordfhip
" with fo much Levity, even when you
" wou'd appear to be ferious, gives me,
" I confefs, the greateft Aftonifhment.
" What Guilt? 'Tis ftrange, 'tis very
" ftrange, that this fhou'd e'er be made
" a Queftion. Wou'd you but take a-
                              " nother

" 'nother View of things, and a little
" turn the Scale, you'd wonder at your
" felf for making it ; all that Varniſh and
" Paint of Words, with which, it at
" preſent ſeems ſo well gloſs'd, wou'd
" with abundance of eaſe be then ſeen
" through, and appear a Poor Umbrage
" to ſhade the baſeneſs that lurks there-
" in. Think what Thoughts you wou'd
" have of this, were you to take your
" Ladies part ; how wou'd you (I am
" willing to ſpeak ſoftly) blame her In-
" conſtancy in the moſt paſſionate terms,
" and when you took a View of the
" Curs'd Ingratitude of him, who was
" the Partner of her Crime, what
" Names are there ſo juſtly reproach-
" ful, that you wou'd not load him
" withal. How wou'd it with Reaſon
" Incenſe you to have it ask'd, whether
" Heaven gave us Appetites, only to be
" reſtrain'd ? And might not this with
" equal Reaſon be ſaid ? Have not
" Women the ſame Appetites as Men ?
" Our *Meſſalina's* ; nay, every common
" Proſtitute, too plainly ſpeak, what I
                              " wou'd

" wou'd otherwife willingly conceal in
" this Cafe ; But wou'd this give you
" Satisfaction?   No! then wou'd you
" urge,   urge with the juft Refentment
" of one, whofe Wrongs are not to be
" repair'd, that as Heaven gave us Ap-
" petites, it gave us Reafon alfo to go-
" vern them ; aggravate with the keen-
" eft Energy ; the Treachery, Perjury,
" and every other Odium,   a Crime fo
" foul carries with it.   We Women, I
" confefs, never gain'd much Reputa-
" tion by our Oratory ; but this is a
" a Theme fo natural, fo very eafy, that
" even a Woman can't want Elocution
" in in't :   The Rage and Fury that
" Fires your Breaft, when only a bare
" Sufpicion of this kind has enter'd, is
" what none can be Ignorant of : That
" Jealoufy, bare Jealoufy, is the Rage
" of Man,   not only the Proverb, but
" all Hiftory has prov'd ; what fhall we
" fay then, when the Fact is open, and
" the raging Fury of the Mind, can no
" longer properly be call'd Jealoufy ?
" Not only the Impetuous Fury of pri-
                                   " vate

"vate Refentment, but the Common
" Suffrage of the cooleft and moft deli-
" berate Reafon of Mankind in gene-
" ral, gives the Anfwer ; Adultery! is
" a Crime fo hainous in the Eye of all
" Nations, that they have been at a lofs,
" what Punifhment to allot it. I am
" not fo well Vers'd in Theory to make
" particular Quotations ; but when the
" Fact was flagrant, that the Perfons
" Convicted were to be Burnt, Ston'd,
" and put to feveral other, Violent and
' Ignominious Deaths, by the general
" and uncontefted Laws, not only of
' God, but of almoft all the polifh'd Nati-
' ons in the World, is a Truth, my fmall
" Reading has made known to me. It
" is confefs'd, it may be faid, notwith-
" ftanding, they that made thefe Laws
" did not believe it a Crime, and when
" Gentlemen are refolv'd to be fo witty,
" who can anfwer them? This, we can
" fay, he that denies the Sun to be a
" glorious Object, when at Noon it
" fhines out in its full Luftre, ought to
" be made to ftare on it, 'till the Weak-
" nefs

" nefs of his Eyes, quite Baffles, the
" Perverfenefs of his Will. And we may
" venture further to fay, as long as thofe
" very Gentlemen are fo fenfibly touch'd
" when they find what they fo ftrenu-
" oufly inculcated to others, turn'd up-
" on themfelves, and that none are
" readier at fuch Times to exagerate
" the Greatnefs of the Injury. As long
" as the yet more cool and deliberate
" Senfe of Mankind, continues to de-
" clare it felf fo warmly againft it ; and
" *Laftly,* as long as that innate Senfe
" of Vertue, Honour, and Reafon which
" mov'd them thereto, bares any Sway in
" the World ; Adultery will be efteem'd
" a Guilt of the blackeft, and moft hate-
" ful Nature.

    " So that after all, the Crimes I fear'd,
" are not fo trifling and imagmary, as
" your Lordfhip is pleas'd to reprefent
" them : And tho' you wou'd feem to
" draw this conclufion, even from the
" Decree of Heaven it felf :   Yet I can't
" but obferve the Senfe you are forc'd
" for that purpofe to fix thereon, is fo
                         " apparently

" apparently ſtrain'd, and againſt the
" moſt evident experience of all Man-
" kind, that it carries its own Convicti-
" on along with it. He muſt have made
" very little Obſervation of the World,
" that does not know Licentiouſneſs of
" this kind, is Fruitful of nothing but
" Diſeaſes : And were People Univer-
" ſally to indulge themſelves therein,
" a very ſmall time wou'd diſplay the
" whole Earth as void of Inhabitants,
" as of Honour and Vertue: Nothing
" but wild Confuſion and brutal Fury,
" wou'd Ravage through the World,
" and all the moſt endearing Tyes of
" Nature, Blood, Kindred, Society and
" every thing elſe, that is truely engaging
" wou'd be miſerably trampl'd under
" Foot. And wou'd this be to fulfil the
" Commands of Heaven ! Wou'd this
" be to repleniſh the Earth ! Where
" wou'd be the endearing Names of
" Husband and Wife ? Where the ve-
" nerable ones of Father and Mother,
" Brother and Siſter, with the nume-
" rous other happy Appellations, that

M " now

" now juftly delight the World? What
" wou'd become of thofe noble diftincti-
" ons of Blood and Quality, your Lord-
" fhip, has fuch particular Reafon to
" glory in ; or indeed of every other
" Diftinction that is truely Praife wor-
" thy ; if once, what you have fo unhap-
" pily contended for, be receiv'd in the
" World? All wou'd be miferably loft,
" confounded and forgotten. Appe-
" tite wou'd refume the Seat of Reafon,
" and the wild Extravagances it wou'd
" inceffantly run us into, wou'd debafe
" us below the Beafts that perifh. If
" this be the Courage, the Pleafure,
" you recommend ; may I ever be
" charg'd with Melancholly and Cow-
" ardice. If there be none magnani-
" mous, but fuch as can brave Damna-
" tion, I fhall never envy their Cou-
" rage. Whatever Pride fome may take,
" being witty, above the fober Reafon
" of Mankind ; and amufing the World
" with their wild and novel Notions:
" For my Part, I had rather, as you
" love to call it, be hagg'd by the idle
                          " Superfti-

" Superſtition of the Mob ; than by en-
" deavouring to advance the Reputati-
" on of my Parts, in the Methods you
" propoſe, get the Stamp of a Wit af-
" fixt to my Character. I can't eaſily
" forget, My Lord, how fatal this Sort
" of Vanity, prov'd to our firſt Parents.
" You ſhall be like Gods, was the Lan-
" guage of the Fiend, when his Deſign
" was to make them Devils. This is
" an old Bait, and therefore I wonder
" you did not ſo far reflect on the Origi-
" nal Smart, it gave us, as to think I'd
" be, however a little Cautious on that
" Score, how I ſwallow'd it a-freſh.
" No, My Lord ! how great ſoever the
" Deſire of Knowledge may be in me,
" I'll never buy it at that Price. Be-
" ſides, wholly to be led by the Bent of
" a wild, and extravagant Apetite,
" ſeems, to me, as mean, and inglori-
" ous, as 'tis deteſtable and pernicious.
" 'Tis below the Reaſon of Man, and
" and is ſo far from raiſing his Genius,
" above the Reſt of his Species, that it
" meerly deſtroys all that's Noble, and

M 2   " Manly

" Manly, in his Soul ; and makes him
" the meaneſt, the vileſt Slave in the
" World.　If the giving a Looſe to the
" moſt ignoble, irregular Deſires of hu-
" mane Nature,　be a diſtinguiſhing
" Mark of our Senſe ;　not only the
" Scum, and Refuſe of Humanity,　but
" the very Beaſts are upon the Level with
" us.　Nay ! upon your own Principles,
" they'd out-vie you ; for as their Re-
" flection is leſs, their Guſt is ſtronger ;
" they are void of thoſe bodeing Fears,
" which, as long as you are ſubject to
" the leaſt Sallies of Reaſon, muſt wrack
" your Breaſt : In ſpight of all your
" diſſembl'd Gaiety, ſomething gloomy
" will hang over your Souls ; Debau-
" chery ! will ever carry its own Ne-
" meſis along with it ; and tho' its un-
" happy Proſelites may ſeem to ſwim in
" in continual Delight ; yet there is al-
" ways ſome latent Wormwood, ever
" imbitters all their Enjoyments. They
" may talk indeed often, of, I know not
" what Romantic Sort of Felicity ; but
" wou'd they be ingenious, I'm very
　　　　　　　　　　　　　　" ſure

" fure, they muft own (in all the Courfe
" of their Extravagancies) they never
" yet experienc'd it. No, nor never,
" never will ; hunt after it they may,
" but will ever find it a fruitlefs Toil,
" Vexation, Remorfe, Difappointment,
" Difeafes and Death, are what they
" are fure to find ; but Pleafure, Satis-
" faction, are what will ever fly them.
" And fo it muft, it will ever be ; Hip-
" pinefs ! Satisfaction ! is the peculiar
" Reward of Vertue ; and he that ex-
" pects to find it any where elfe, only
" mocks his Reafon, and wracks his
" Soul with Difappointments. Heaven
" has decreed it fo, and the Experience
" of all the World has prov'd it irrever-
" fible. Do but try, My Lord ; I'm
" fure you'll blefs your Choice, and me
" that prompt you to it. The Joy, the
" inward Complacency, that will in-
" ceffantly regale your Breaft, will be
" fuch as can only be felt ; no Words can
" reach it, 'tis fomething fo fublime that
" it cannot be utter'd. You'll find it a
" Spring of Pleafure, never to be exhau-

" fted,

" fted, free from that Satiety, that Sur-
" feit, that ever before us'd to pall your
" moft abftracted Enjoyments, and fo
" far exempted from the bitter Stings
" that follow them ; that you'll find it's
" every Way, a Way of Pleafantnefs, and
" all its Paths are Peace. Ceafe then any
" longer to purfue, the loofe Defires of
" a bafe, and ignoble Appetite ; and
" refolve, for the future, to act up to the
" Dignity of your Reafon and Cha-
" racter ; make your felf but once fen-
" fible of the Bleffings, Heaven has al-
" read put into your Hands ; and then
" you'll be fatisfy'd, you need not go
" from Home for any fort of Happinefs.
" Happinefs is an inbred Quality, and
" vainly fought in any Thing, but the
" Reflections of a Mind untainted with
" Guilt. This, this alone, is a conti-
" nual Feaft, and gives a Guft to every
" Thing we do ; and wou'd Your Lord-
" fhip be perfuaded once to make the Ex-
" periment, it wou'd Crown your whole
" Life with more fubftantial Glories,
" than the greateft Monarch on Earth,
" ever

" ever yet enjoy'd ; 'twou'd make you
" more than Conqueror, and fill your
" Soul with that juſt Contempt of your
" former, miſtaken Notions of Happi-
" neſs, as wou'd abundantly enhance
" the Satisfaction of your Mind, in the
" preſent Felicity you poſſeſs. A chear-
" ful Vigor wou'd diffuſe it ſelf through
" all your Veins, and the continual
" Soundneſs, and Health of your Body
" every Day give you freſh Evidences,
" of the Folly, as well as Miſery of the
" Luxurious. Then wou'd you be happily
" inform'd, that Love is a Paſſion of a pure
" and etherial Birth, not nurs'd by the
" Fumes of heated and diſtemper'd Blood ;
" but altogether ſuſtain'd, by the ſweet
" Endearments of a happy and noble Har-
" mony of Souls : Experiment. Alone,
" in the winning Careſſes of your Lady's
" Beauty, and Inocence ; thoſe Plea-
" ſures, you ſo vainly ſought elſewhere.
" With her, you might truly wanton
" your Hours away, not only in ſoft,
" but inocent Delight. Delight ! wor-
" thy the Dignity, the Reaſon of hu-
" mane

" mane Nature; free, entirely free, from
" the bitter Alloy of Remorse in Frui-
" tion, and the wracking Pains of a
" diftemper'd Mass of Blood in the
" Confequence. Here you might, in
" Realty, be as free as Air, and un-
" confin'd as Thought; free from the
" vileft Slavery in the World, that of
" an exorbitant, and ungovern'd Luft;
" and abridg'd of nothing, but what
" wou'd furely make you miferable.
" Let me therefore intreat you, by all
" that is great and ingenious, in hu-
" mane Nature, all that is noble, and
" generous in your Breaft, by the Ino-
" cence, Beauty, and every other Charm,
" that fo refplendantly fhines in your
" Lady, by all the facred Ties, both of
" Vows and Affection; you, and thofe
" of Gratitude and Humanity, I lie
" under to her; by all the Hopes you
" have, of conveying your Name and
" Honours, to diftant Profterity; in
" fine, as you tender, either the Health
" of your Body, or Salvation of your
" Soul; be prevail'd on, henceforth
" ever

"ever to abandon such mean, such ig-
"noble Desires; and firmly resolve, at
"once, to bless your self, your Lady,
"Posterity, and every Thing else, that
"is, or ought to be dear to you, with
"the purest, the most substantial Hap-
"piness of this Life; and live up to the
"not imaginary, licentious, but real
"Dignity of humane Nature.

Dorinda, here putting a Period to her
Harangue, found the Scene quite rever-
s'd in *Phylopones.* Those mean, lascivious Airs, that before took up his
whole Countenance, now seem'd to
give Way to something more generous
and Manly in his Soul, and every Look
he gave her, evidently show'd he was
no longer able to bare up against her.
So powerfully had, what she had said,
impress'd his Soul; that he was no
longer asham'd to own himself entirely
baffl'd; nay, he took a sort of Pride in
acknowledging her Conquest, and never thought he cou'd expatiate sufficiently thereon. And indeed, ever after,

M 5   by

by all his Actions, so fully indicated the Sincerity of his Conversion, as entirely satisfy'd her, she need fear no further Molestation from him. All his former irregular Passions, were now turn'd into the profoundest Deference, and Respect; and he was so far from making any further Attempts on her Modesty, that he ever after treated, and spoke to her, as if she had been something more than humane.

Leaving *Dorinda* thus gloriously triumphant over both the loose Desires and Principles of her young lustful Antagonist; we'll now pay a Visit to her old Friend *Panaretus,* who having now gone through the several Fatigues of a Campaign, naturally calls for our notice. To entertain you with the several Particulars of his Exploits in his Military Capacity, may be esteem'd an invidious Detraction from the Performances of some, on whom the *Gazzet* has thought fitter to father them, and therefore, since he was only a private Captain, we

shall

shall venture only to tell you, that after he had diftinguish'd his Courage in the moft shocking Dangers of one Engagement, and two Sieges, he embark'd, and arriv'd safe at *Harwich.* At his landing, being welcom'd on Shore by fome of his Comrades, with a pretty plentiful Glafs, it caus'd him to be very late at Night, before he, and his Serjeant, who accompany'd him, fet out for *London,* which he was now very defirous of feeing, but a very odd Accident happening by the Way, confiderably retarded his Journey.

They had not rode above half an Hour, but (the Night being exceeding dark, and their Heads fomething fluster'd with what they had drank) they found themfelves wholly loft in their Way. How to fet themfelves right again, they found wholly impoffible; looking therefore round about them to fee if they cou'd fpy out any Houfe, after they had vainly rambl'd about a Quarter of an Hour longer, *Panaretus* fpy'd, ſpy'd, about half a Mile diſtant from them, the light of a Candle, whereupon he immediately commenc'd a Reſolution of making up to the Place where it was The Confuſion they were both before in, and the Deſire they had of putting an End, for that Night, to their Journey, made them quickly get up to the Houſe, where they had at firſt deſcry'd the Candle, and having upon a nearer Scrutiny found it to be the Country-Seat of ſome Nobleman. *Panaretus* (finding they were like to be expos'd all Night to the Weather, unleſs he took up a Reſolution that was ſomething extraordinary) order'd his Serjeant to go and knock at the Door, and tell them their Caſe; bidding him further, if he cou'd, to prevail on them, to give them a Night's Lodging. *Will.* (for that was his Serjeant's Name) having receiv'd his Inſtructions, was not at all to ſeek in his Story. Going therefore to the Door, with that Aſſurance that had bore him out in many a worſe Brunt than this, very coura-

geouſly

geoufly knocks thereat; upon which, having his Bufinefs demanded, by the Porter, he told him, " He was a Ser- " vant of a Gentleman, who fat hard " by on his Horfe, benighted; and was " come from him, to requeft the Fa- " vour of his Lord, of a Night's Lodg- " ing. The Porter having receiv'd this Intelligence, immediately communica- ted it to another of his fellow Servants, in order to acquaint his Lord therewith, who being inform'd of *Panaretus*'s De- fire, inftantly gave Orders he fhou'd be kindly conducted in. *Will.* being in- form'd of this, immediately went and told his Mafter the fuccefs of his Em- bafly; and having convey'd him fafe to the Door, left him to make his own Apology. *Panaretus* being conducted by one of the Footmen, into the Pre- fence of his Lord, immediately exprefs'd himfelf with that well-bred Gratitude, as made him not at all repent his Ho- fpitality. The Night being too far fpent to admit of much Converfe, after a fhort Repaft, *Panaretus* was conducted up

to an agreeable Lodging, where immediately unrigging, he was left, by his
Attendant, free to take his Repofe.
In the Interim, his Man *Will.* was fo
fully taken up with telling his Fighting-
Stories, and partaking of the Libe-
rality of his Audience, the gaping Cook
and Butler, that between Eating, Suck-
ing, and Lying, he did not go to Bed
all Night. But to return to his Mafter.

Panaretus having been in his Bed a-
bout half an Hour, plainly perceiv'd,
from the next Room, which was only
parted with a thin Partition, two Ladies talking together, and by his ftrictly attending to the Sound, to his Aftonifhment, heard the following Words
from one of them, *viz.* "I hope, Ma-
"dam, you'll excufe my Boldnefs, (fince
"we are neither of us inclin'd, at pre-
"fent, to fleep) if I prefs you to pro-
"fecute the reft of the Story, of what
"pafs'd between you and *Panaretus.*
I need not tell you, the hearing his
own Name mention'd in a Place he was
an utter Stranger to, gave his Ears a
very

very rouzing Alarm. But let it fuffice, to acquaint you, that no fooner had he fix'd himfelf to give a fteady Attentention to the Iffue of thefe, at prefent, fo very myfterious Expreffions, but he cou'd plainly diftinguifh the Voice of *Dorinda* her felf, recounting all the Particulars of their Walk in the *Spring-Gardens*, with the Adventure with the *Frenchmen*, and *Phylaftratus*, in the *Park*, *Play-Houfe*, &c. with all the particular Endearments that had pafs'd between them, to her coming there; with the manner of that, even to the minuteft Circumftance. A Difcovery of this furprizing Nature, made *Panaretus* an utter ftranger to Sleep: The kind Providence that had ftrangely brought him hither to make it, was what he cou'd not but gratefully acknowledge; but that which abundantly more engag'd his Thanks to Almighty Goodnefs, was the care it had taken of *Dorinda* fince his Abfence; this was a Reflection he cou'd not but largely defcant upon; but before the feveral Tranfports of his
Soul

Soul cou'd fettle into any thing like a
Refolution how to act, an Accident, if
poffible, more odd than any had yet
happen'd, gave him frefh Amufement.

Dorinda having, at Requeft of Mrs.
Betty, her Bed fellow, finifhed her Narrative, found her felf, on a fudden,
under fuch an Indifpofition, as oblig'd
her to rife, and go into the Garden :
Now at her return, *Panaretus*'s Room,
being next to hers, having no Light,
and his Door being open, through miftake, fhe went directly into his Room,
and thinking fhe was in her own, immediately got into Bed to *Panaretus*,
and clung very clofe to him, telling
him, It was very cold. *Panaretus*,
knowing by her Voice, it was *Dorinda*, who through miftake was come into his Bed inftead of her own, immediately embracing in his Arms, told
her, " 'Twas very kindly done of her,
" indeed, to come and accompany a
" poor Traveller fo. *Dorinda* finding
her felf in the Arms, (as fhe thought)
of a ftrange Gentleman, was furpriz'd
almoft

almoſt to Diſtraction : She omitted no
Words ; no Tears, to move him to let
her go, urging over and over the Unhappineſs of her Miſtake ; largely inculcating how ungenerous 'twou'd be
in him, to take the Advantages of it.
Panaretus, for his Part, ſeem'd altogether inexorable; and, in fine, for half
an Hour together, gabbl'd to her, all
that his Wit and Fancy cou'd furniſh,
offering, however, no violence to her,
till finding her plead ſo hard, and grieve
her ſelf ſo much, as he fear'd wou'd
do her a Diskindneſs afterwards in her
Health. He told her, " If ſhe wou'd
" promiſe him One Thing, he wou'd
" let her go. *Dorinda* ſeeing him a little inclin'd to treat, told him, ſhe'd
comply with any thing that lay in her
power, on that Condition, and therefore deſir'd him to make his Propoſal.
" I am then, ſaid *Panaretus,* a young
" Captain, juſt return'd from *Flanders,*
" by my Induſtry in my Office I have
" got about a Thouſand Pound, now
" you need not be told how great a
                              " ſtranger

" ſtranger you are to me; but if you
" will conſent to be my wedded Wife,
" I'll have you, let your Circumſtan-
" ces be what they will. The Gene-
" roſity of your Offer, ſaid *Dorinda,* is
" what I cannot but acknowledge, but
" muſt pardon me, if I tell you, your
" Propoſal is what I can't poſſibly a-
" gree with. I am engag'd already in
" that kind, and therefore hope, on
" that Conſideration, you'll excuſe me;
" require any thing of me that is not
" inconſiſtent with my Faith and Ho-
" nour, and you ſhall find the moſt
" ready Creature in the World to per-
" form it. *Panaretus,* after he had
ſeem'd to preſs his Propoſal on her
with all the Earneſtneſs in the World;
finding his detaining her, griev'd and
perplex'd her exceedingly, with abundance of ſeeming Reluctancy, at laſt
told her, " If ſhe'd promiſe to let him
" ſee her in the Morning, he'd let her go.
Dorinda return'd him abundance of
Thanks for his Generoſity, and ſtrictly
promiſing he ſhou'd ſee her next Morning,

ing, was difmifs'd by him from the moft
hateful Confinement, as fhe then tho't,
fhe ever fuftain'd in her Life.

After fhe had left him, fhe immediately went to her old Bed-fellow,
who had been in fad pain for her fo
long abfence ; but when fhe came to
be acquainted with the reafon of it,
was as much diverted. The Thoughts
of her having been in Bed with a Man,
convey'd fo many pretty Ideas into
Mrs. *Betty*'s Fancy, that fhe knew not
how to abandon them. *Dorinda,* indeed, told her Story in a very difmal
Accent ; but, do what fhe cou'd, fhe
cou'd, not prevail on her Affociate to
pity her ; nothing was to be got from
her but Interrogatives, as, *What did
be fay then? How did be take it? Did
not be feem angry?* and the like, till
the whole Night was fpent by them
both, without a Wink of Sleep.

As to *Panaretus,* he, indeed, was upon the Level, with refpect to Sleep ;
but,

but, however, fpent his Time in more
material Reflections. The unfhaken
Conftancy of *Dorinda* was what afforded
him as much Delight, as the Thoughts
of having light on her fo very providen-
tially : But that which yet made a more
pleafing Impreffion of his Imagination,
was the Thoughts of that pleafing Surprize it wou'd give her when in the
Morning fhe came to know 'twas him
fhe was in Bed with. Having fpun
out the Time with thefe and the like
Reflections ; the Dawn of the Morning
beginning to make confiderable advances, he jump'd out of his Bed, and ad-
jufting his Military Habilements as well
as he cou'd, pofted himfelf to a Win-
dow that look'd into the Garden, in
order to fee if he cou'd not fpy *Dorinda* walking there, eafily collecting fhe
wou'd not fleep over-found that Night,
no more than he. He had not been
long at his Poft, but, agreeable to his
Conjecture, he fpy'd a young Female
tripping it along one of the Grafs-Plats,
who was prefently follow'd by *Dorinda* ;

da, for the Thoughts of what had paſt being too powerful on Mrs. *Betty's* Fancy, to let her lie without kicking in her Bed ; after ſome Perſuaſion, ſhe prevail'd on *Dorinda* to get up, and take a Walk in the Garden, in order to hear a yet fuller Account of the Night's- Adventure. No ſooner had *Panaretus* ſet his Eyes on her, but he was enflam'd with the moſt ardent Deſire of ſpeaking to her ; ſallying therefore out of his Chamber, and tracing their Steps to the Garden- Door, he immediately proceeded to take a Circuit round the Garden, in order to give them the more ſurprize when they met him. Sculking therefore behind the Hedges, that they might not perceive him, before he had a mind, he had ſoon an Opportunity of popping upon them juſt at the turning of a Corner, which inſtantly embracing, at the very Juncture as they turn'd a Corner to go into another Path ; he preſented himſelf before them, with all the Cheatfulneſs imaginable, giving them both

both a *Good Morrow*. Mrs. *Betty*, whofe
Mind was before, by her Bed-fellows
Story, altogether taken up in Contem-
plations on Man ; feeing *Panaretus* a
pretty young Fellow, was immediately
ready to return his Compliment, with
the ufual Pertnefs. and Levity, that the
Opinion fhe had of her own Wit, and
pretty Face, never fail'd to furnifh her
with : But turning her felf to *Dorinda*,
to her furprize, found her Task was
rather to keep her from fwooning, than
to Dialogue it with him. For the fo
furprizing and unexpected fight of *Panaretus*, had fo powerfully lock'd up all
her Senfes in Tranfport, that fhe ftood
a confiderable time unable to fpeak a
Word ; but, at laft, the Powers of her
Soul having a little refum'd their wonted regular Courfe, and the Organs of
Speech the Capacity of Utterance ; eagerly flinging her felf in his Arms, fhe
broke out in thefe Expreffions. "Oh!
" *Panaretus*, be thou a *Spectrum*, or what-
" ever elfe the filly Vulgar do fright
" themfelves withal. This I am fure
" of,

" of, any Thing that bears a Form fo
" lovely as thine, can never be hurtful
" to me: I will, I muſt embrace thee,
" tho' the daring Act ſhou'd immedi-
" ately ſtrike me dead. A *Spectrum!*
Anſwer'd *Panaretus*, " No, no, believe
" me, I'm Fleſh and Bones; and tho'
" when you reflect on laſt Night's Ad-
" venture, you'll be apt to conclude I
" have not much Blood, yet, I can aſ-
" ſure you, what I have is pure good,
" and that's more than One young Fel-
" low, that wears a Red-Coat, in Ten
" can ſay. I ſhou'd ſpin theſe Papers
out to a fine length, ſhou'd I here endeavour to recount all the Endearments,
both in Words and Actions, that paſs'd
between them. After therefore *Panaretus* had fully acquainted her with all
the Particulars of his Adventures, ſince
his Abſence; and droll'd on her, for
telling in the Bed ſhe was engag'd to
another; adding further, She need not
tell him by what means ſhe came thither, becauſe he heard her fully recount them to the young Lady, her
Bed-

Bed-fellow, as he lay in his Bed. Having spent an Hour or two in thus diverting her and himself, they agreed Mrs. *Betty* shou'd go and tell *Phylopones*, and his Lady, the happy News, that they also might bear a part in the Joy.

Phylopones, and his Lady, having, agreeable to this Refolution, receiv'd a thorough Intelligence of the furprizing Particulars of what had pafs'd, from Mrs. *Betty*, immediately reforted to the Arbour, where she had left them, to congratulate their fo happy and furprifing Meeting. Nothing but univerfal Joy difplay'd it felf in the Countenance of all the House, on this Occafion. *Phylopones* told them, He was refolv'd they shou'd honour his House with the Celebration of their Nuptials; and his Lady added, She shou'd lie with *Panaretus* once again, in the fame Bed, and not plead her Engagements to any other. In short, fo ftrange was their Importunity, and weak the Oppofition our Lovers made thereto, that the very Day

was

was then fixt, wherein *Hymen* was to do his Part.

The so long wish'd for Consummation of our Generous Pairs Happiness, now making very near advances, *Panaretus* acquainted *Dorinda,* That he thought himself oblig'd to give his Father, and Friend *Phylastratus,* an Account of his Nuptials, and to invite the latter to them; to which she immediately agreeing, enclos'd in a Letter to his Father, he sent his Friend *Phylastratus* the following Lines, *viz.*

GENEROUS FRIEND,

I Doubt not it will strangely surprize you, to find the first News you receive from me, at my return from a hazardous Campaign, an Invitation to my Wedding. But so it is, Heaven yet designs to make me happy, in the best Wife in the World: This Day Seven-night, therefore Dorinda *and I desire your Company at the Celebration of our Nuptials. The astonishing*

N

Series

Series of Providence, that has brought this about, the Bearer will fully inform you of. We both depend on your Company, and he that brings you this Paper, will conduct you to us. In the Interim we remain your affectionate Friends, and humble Servants,

Panaretus *and* Dorinda.

Panaretus having wrote thefe Two Letters, got leave of *Phylopones* to let one of his Footmen carry them to his Father, and Friend; and having given him full Inftructions what to fay to them both, difmifs'd him to profecute his Meffage.

The Diligence of our Courrier having foon convey'd the Letters into the Hands of the Perfons they were directed to: *Phylaftratus* at once delighted and aftonifh'd at the News the Letter and its Bearer brought him, immediately prepar'd himfelf to follow his Guide. The Defire he had of being prefent, at fo happy a Solemnity, gave Wings to his fpeed, fo that his ready Appearance put them quickly out of all Fears of wanting his Company.

Every Thing being thus happily ad-jufted to the Wifhes of our Couple, and the Morn now come, that was to give *Dorinda* the Name of *Bride*, with all the fplendid Triumph of Love and Joy, fhe was led to the Chappel, where that happy Union of Hearts and Souls, that had fo long been commenc'd, be-tween her, and her belov'd *Panaretus*, was publickly ratify'd by their joining Hands. The moft enlarg'd Courtefie and Generofity were exerted on this happy Occafion, both by *Phylopones* and his Lady: They feem'd to emulate each other in the good Offices they did them; kept publick Feftivities for their Nup-tials feveral Days together; and fo ex-traordinary was the Munificence there-of, in every Inftance, that it rais'd the Admiration of all the Country round them.

N 2 Having

Having thus liv'd under the happy Influences of their Noble Benefactors Generofity, a full Month fince their Marriage; the reciprocal Defire they had of feeing their Native Abode, made them now begin to entreat, that they might return to *London*. Great. was the Reluctancy was fhown before this cou'd be granted; but *Panaretus* urging feveral Reafons, that render'd it necef- fary. After the moft folemn Affurances of Friendfhip, and mutual Correfpon- dence for the future, were given on both Sides, *Panaretus*, *Dorinda*, and *Phy- laftratus*, parted with them, and took their Journey directly to *London*.

The News of *Panaretus* and *Dorinda*'s fo happy and furprizing Marriage ha- ving reach'd the Ears of *Vulpone*, be- fore they arriv'd: He no fooner re- flected on his former Deportment, but was alarm'd with a thoufand perplex- ing Fears. The Thoughts of having to do with. an injur'd and incens'd Lawyer,

Lawyer, run him into Convulſions: Tho' he cou'd very willingly, without ſo much as making a wry Face, have before ſwallow'd all that he had of *Dorinda's,* yet now he was willing to be very honeſt; the Scene was quite chang'd, and the fear of paying a long Bill of Charges, made him the moſt tractable Creature in the World. He had an utter Averſion to all Writings but *Bonds,* and they too very little delighted him, without they bore the Intereſt of *Thirty per Cent.* Under theſe terrible Apprehenſions therefore, he immediately reſolves, and accordingly goes to *Panaretus's* Father, freely offering to come to account, and refund what he had of *Dorinda's;* entreating him, with all the ſervile Meaneſs of an alarm'd and frighten'd Avarice, to prevail on his Son, not to put him to any Charges in Law; which, being immediately comply'd with, *Panaretus* was no ſooner come, but, amongſt other Things, had the Diverſion to find what a Fright he had put his old Antagoniſt in; and that he

had

had anticipated even his asking for that, he thought he muſt have been forc'd to contend very warmly for.

Having thus fully ſettled all their Affairs, without the leaſt Interruption, they retir'd to a convenient Country-Seat, not above five Miles diſtant from *London*; more fully to proſecute thoſe rais'd Enjoyments, which are the peculiar Bleſſing of a chaſt and regular Affection. Many were the Years they paſs'd together, each being crown'd with Heaven's diſtinguiſhing Favours: Happy, very happy the Iſſue of their Bodies; and, in ſhort, every Inſtance of their Lives was a glorious Demonſtration, *That Happineſs, real ſubſtantial Happineſs, is only to be found in* Innocence *and* Vertue.

F I N I S.